# DESPAIR

BOOKS BY *Vladimir Nabokov*

NOVELS

*Mary*

*King, Queen, Knave*

*The Defense*

*The Eye*

*Glory*

*Laughter in the Dark*

*Despair*

*Invitation to a Beheading*

*The Gift*

*The Real Life of Sebastian Knight*

*Bend Sinister*

*Lolita*

*Pnin*

*Pale Fire*

*Ada or Ardor: A Family Chronicle*

*Transparent Things*

*Look at the Harlequins!*

SHORT FICTION

*Nabokov's Dozen*

*A Russian Beauty and Other Stories*

*Tyrants Destroyed and Other Stories*

*Details of a Sunset and Other Stories*

*The Enchanter*

DRAMA

*The Waltz Invention*

*Lolita: A Screenplay*

*The Man from the USSR and Other Plays*

AUTOBIOGRAPHY AND INTERVIEWS

*Speak, Memory: An Autobiography Revisited*

*Strong Opinions*

# DESPAIR

A NOVEL BY

# VLADIMIR NABOKOV

VINTAGE INTERNATIONAL
VINTAGE BOOKS   A DIVISION OF RANDOM HOUSE, INC.
NEW YORK

First Vintage International Edition, May 1989

A somewhat briefer version of this novel originally appeared
in *Playboy*.

Library of Congress Cataloging-in-Publication Data
Nabokov, Vladimir Vladimirovich, 1899–1977.
Despair: a novel.
(Vintage international)
Translation of: Otchaianie.
Originally published: New York : G.P. Putnam's Sons, 1966.
I. Title.
PG3476.N3083    1989    813′.54    88-40533
ISBN 0-679-72343-9 (pbk.)

Manufactured in the United States of America
10

*To Véra*

# Foreword

The Russian text of *Despair* (*Otchayanie*—a far more sonorous howl) was written in 1932, in Berlin. The émigré review *Sovremennye Zapiski*, in Paris, serialized it in the course of 1934, and the émigré publishing house Petropolis, in Berlin, published the book in 1936. As has happened in the case of all my other works, *Otchayanie* (despite Hermann's conjecture) is banned in the prototypical police state.

At the end of 1936, while I was still living in Berlin—where another beastliness had started to megaphone—I translated *Otchayanie* for a London publisher. Although I had been scribbling in English all my literary life in the margin, so to say, of my Russian writings, this was my first serious attempt (not counting a wretched poem in a Cambridge University review, circa 1920) to use English for what may be loosely termed an artistic purpose. The result seemed to me stylistically clumsy, so I asked a rather grumpy Englishman, whose services I obtained through an agency in Berlin, to read the stuff; he found a few solecisms in the first chapter, but then refused to continue, saying he disapproved of the book; I suspect he wondered if it might not have been a true confession.

In 1937 John Long Limited, of London, brought out *Despair* in a convenient edition with a *catalogue raisonné* of their publications at the back. Despite that bonus, the book sold badly, and a few years later a German bomb destroyed the entire stock. The only copy extant is, as far as I know, the one I own—but two or three may still be lurking amidst abandoned reading matter on the dark shelves of seaside boarding houses from Bournemouth to Tweedmouth.

For the present edition I have done more than revamp my thirty-year-old translation: I have revised *Otchayanie* itself. Lucky students who may be able to compare the three texts will also note the addition of an important passage which had been stupidly omitted in more timid times. Is this fair, is this wise from a scholar's point of view? I can readily imagine what Pushkin might have said to his trembling paraphrasts; but I also know how pleased and excited I would have been in 1935 had I been able to foreread this 1965 version. The ecstatic love of a young writer for the old writer he will be some day is ambition in its most laudable form. This love is not reciprocated by the older man in his larger library, for even if he does recall with regret a naked palate and a rheumless eye, he has nothing but an impatient shrug for the bungling apprentice of his youth.

*Despair*, in kinship with the rest of my books, has no social comment to make, no message to bring in its teeth. It does not uplift the spiritual organ of man, nor does it show humanity the right exit. It contains far fewer "ideas" than do those rich vulgar novels that are acclaimed so hysterically in the short echo-walk between the ballyhoo and the hoot. The attractively shaped object or Wiener-schnitzel dream that the eager Freudian may think he distinguishes in the remoteness of my wastes will turn out to be on closer inspection a derisive mirage organized by my agents. Let me add, just in case, that experts on literary "schools" should wisely refrain this time from casually dragging in "the influence of German Impressionists": I do not know German and have never read the Impressionists—whoever they are. On the other hand, I do know French and shall be interested to see if anyone calls my Hermann "the father of existentialism."

The book has less White-Russian appeal than have my other émigré novels; * hence it will be less puzzling and irritating to those readers who have been brought up on the leftist propaganda of the thirties. Plain readers, on the other hand, will welcome its plain structure and pleasing plot—which, however, is not quite as familiar as the writer of the rude letter in Chapter Eleven assumes it to be.

There are many entertaining conversations throughout the book, and the final scene with Felix in the wintry woods is of course great fun.

I am unable to foresee and to fend inevitable attempts to find in the alembics of *Despair* something of the rhetorical venom that I injected into the narrator's tone in a much later novel. Hermann and Humbert are alike only in the sense that two dragons painted by the same artist at different periods of his life resemble each other. Both are neurotic scoundrels, yet there is a green lane in Paradise where Humbert is permitted to wander at dusk once a year; but Hell shall never parole Hermann.

The line and fragments of lines Hermann mutters in Chapter Four come from Pushkin's short poem addressed to his wife in the eighteen-thirties. I give it here in full, in my own translation, with the retention of measure and rhyme, a course that is seldom advisable—nay, admissible—except at

---

* This did not prevent a Communist reviewer (J. P. Sartre), who devoted in 1939 a remarkably silly article to the French translation of *Despair*, from saying that "both the author and the main character are the victims of the war and the emigration."

a very special conjunction of stars in the firmament of the poem, as obtains here.

> 'Tis time, my dear, 'tis time. The heart demands repose.
> Day after day flits by, and with each hour there goes
> A little bit of life; but meanwhile you and I
> Together plan to dwell ... yet lo! 'tis then we die.
> There is no bliss on earth: there's peace and freedom, though.
> An enviable lot I long have yearned to know:
> Long have I, weary slave, been contemplating flight
> To a remote abode of work and pure delight.

The "remote abode" to which mad Hermann finally scurries is economically located in the Roussillon where three years earlier I had begun writing my chess novel, *The Defense*. We leave Hermann there at the ludicrous height of his discomfiture. I do not remember what happened to him eventually. After all, fifteen other books and twice as many years have intervened. I cannot even recall if that film he proposed to direct was ever made by him.

—VLADIMIR NABOKOV

*March 1, 1965*
*Montreux*

# DESPAIR

# Chapter One

If I were not perfectly sure of my power to write and of my marvelous ability to express ideas with the utmost grace and vividness . . . So, more or less, I had thought of beginning my tale. Further, I should have drawn the reader's attention to the fact that had I lacked that power, that ability, et cetera, not only should I have refrained from describing certain recent events, but there would have been nothing to describe, for, gentle reader, nothing at all would have happened. Silly perhaps, but at least clear. The gift of penetrating life's devices, an innate disposition toward the constant exercise of the creative faculty could alone have enabled me . . . At this point I should have compared the breaker of the law which makes such a fuss over a little spilled blood, with a poet or a stage performer. But as my poor left-handed friend used to put it: philosophic speculation is the invention of the rich. Down with it.

It may look as though I do not know how to start. Funny sight, the elderly gentleman who comes lumbering by, jowl flesh flopping, in a valiant dash for the last bus, which he eventually overtakes but is afraid to board in motion and so, with a sheepish smile, drops back, still going at a trot. Is it that I dare not make the leap? It roars, gathers speed, will presently vanish irrevocably around the corner, the bus, the motorbus, the mighty montibus of my tale. Rather bulky imagery, this. I am still running.

My father was a Russian-speaking German from Reval, where he went to a famous agricultural college. My mother, a pure Russian, came from an old princely stock. On hot summer days, a languid lady in lilac silks, she would recline in her rocking chair, fanning herself, munching chocolate, all the blinds down, and the wind from some new-mown field making them billow like purple sails.

During the war, I was interned as a German subject... jolly bad luck, considering that I had just entered the University of St. Petersburg. From the end of 1914 to the middle of 1919 I read exactly one thousand and eighteen books... kept count of them. On my way to Germany I was stranded for three months in Moscow and got married there. Since 1920, I had been living in Berlin. On the ninth of May 1930, having passed the age of thirty-five...

A slight digression: that bit about my mother was a deliberate lie. In reality, she was a woman of the people, simple and coarse, sordidly dressed in a kind of blouse hanging loose at the waist. I could, of course, have crossed it out, but I purposely leave it there as a sample of one of my essential traits: my light-hearted, inspired lying.

Well, as I was saying, the ninth of May 1930 found me on a business trip to Prague. My business was chocolate. Chocolate is a good thing. There are damsels who like only the bitter kind... fastidious little prigs. (Don't quite see why I write in this vein.)

My hands tremble, I want to shriek or to smash something with a bang. ... This mood is hardly suitable for the bland unfolding of a leisurely tale. My heart is itching, a horrible sensation. Must be calm, must keep my head. No good going

on otherwise. Quite calm. Chocolate, as everybody knows ...
(let the reader imagine here a description of its making). Our
trademark on the wrapper showed a lady in lilac, with a fan.
We were urging a foreign firm on the verge of bankruptcy to
convert their manufacturing process to that of ours to supply
Czechoslovakia, and so that was how I came to be in Prague.
On the morning of the ninth of May I left my hotel in a taxi
which took me ... Dull work recounting all this. Bores me
to death. But yearn as I may to reach the crucial point
quickly, a few preliminary explanations seem necessary. So
let us have done with them: the firm's office happened to be
on the very outskirts of the town and I did not find the fellow
I wanted. They told me he would be back in an hour or so. ...

I think I ought to inform the reader that there has just been
a long interval. The sun has had time to set, touching up on
its way down with sanguine the clouds above the Pyrenean
mountain that so resembles Fujiyama. I have been sitting in a
queer state of exhaustion, now listening to the rushing and
crashing of the wind, now drawing noses in the margin of
the page, now slipping into a vague slumber, and then starting up all aquiver. And again there would grow in me that
prickly feeling, that unendurable twitter ... and my will
lay limp in an empty world. ... I had to make a great effort in
order to switch on the light and stick in a new nib. The old
one had got chipped and bent and now looks like the beak
of a bird of prey. No, these are not the throes of creation ...
but something quite different.

Well, as I was saying, the man was out, would be back in
an hour. Having nothing better to do I went for a stroll. It
was a fast, fresh, blue-dappled day; the wind, a distant relation of the one here, winged its course along the narrow
streets; a cloud every now and then palmed the sun, which

reappeared like a conjurer's coin. The public garden, where invalids were hand-pedaling about, was a storm of heaving lilac bushes. I looked at shop signs; picked out some word concealing a Slav root familiar to me, though overgrown with an unfamiliar meaning. I wore new yellow gloves and kept swinging my arms as I rambled on aimlessly. Then all of a sudden the row of houses broke, disclosing a vast stretch of land that at first glance seemed to me most rural and alluring.

After passing some barracks, in front of which a soldier was exercising a white horse, I trod upon soft sticky soil; dandelions trembled in the wind and a shoe with a hole in it was basking in the sunshine under a fence. Farther on, a hill, splendidly steep, sloped up into the sky. Decided to climb it. Its splendor proved to be a deception. Among stunted beeches and elder shrubs a zigzag path with steps hewn into it went up and up. I fancied at first that after the very next turning I should reach a spot of wild and wonderful beauty, but it never showed itself. That drab vegetation could not satisfy me. The shrubs straggled on bare ground, polluted all over with scraps of paper, rags, battered tins. One could not leave the steps of the path, for it dug very deep into the incline; and on either side tree roots and scrags of rotting moss stuck out of its earthen walls like the broken springs of decrepit furniture in a house where a madman had dreadfully died. When at last I reached the summit I found there a few shacks standing awry, a washing line, and on it some pants bloated with the wind's sham life.

I put both elbows on the gnarled wooden railing and, looking down, saw, far below and slightly veiled by mist, the city of Prague; shimmering roofs, smoking chimneys, the barracks I had just passed, a tiny white horse.

Resolving to descend by another way, I took the highroad

which I found beyond the shacks. The only beautiful thing in the landscape was the dome of a gasholder on a hill: round and ruddy against the blue sky, it looked like a huge football. I left the road and began to climb again, this time up a thinly turfed slope. Dreary and barren country. The rattle of a truck came from the road, then a cart passed in the opposite direction, then a cyclist, then, vilely painted rainbowwise, the motor van of a firm of varnishers. In those rascals' spectrum the green band adjoined the red.

For some time I remained gazing at the road from the slope; then turned, went on, found a blurry trail running between two humps of bald ground, and after a while looked about for a place to rest. At some distance from me under a thornbush, flat on his back and with a cap on his face, there sprawled a man. I was about to pass, but something in his attitude cast a queer spell over me: the emphasis of that immobility, the lifelessness of those widespread legs, the stiffness of that half-bent arm. He was dressed in a dark coat and worn corduroy trousers.

"Nonsense," I told myself. "Asleep, merely asleep. No reason for me to intrude." But nevertheless I approached, and with the toe of my elegant shoe flicked the cap off his face.

Trumpets, please! Or still better, that tattoo which goes with a breathless acrobatic stunt. Incredible! I doubted the reality of what I saw, doubted my own sanity, felt sick and faint—honestly I was forced to sit down, my knees were shaking so.

Now, if another had been in my place and had seen what I saw, he might perhaps have burst into roars of laughter. As for me I was too dazed by the mystery implied. While I looked, everything within me seemed to lose hold and come hurtling down from a height of ten stories. I was gazing at a marvel. Its perfection, its lack of cause and object, filled me with a strange awe.

At this point, now that I have got to the important part and quenched the fire of that itching, it is meet, I presume, that I should bid my prose stand at ease and, quietly retracing my steps, try to define my exact mood that morning, and the way my thoughts wandered when, after not finding the firm's agent in, I went for that walk, scaled that hill, stared at the red rotundity of that gasholder against the blue background of a breezy May day. Let us, by all means, settle that matter. So behold me once again before the encounter, bright-gloved but hatless, still loitering aimlessly. What was going on in my mind? Nothing at all, oddly enough. I was absolutely empty and thus comparable to some translucid vessel doomed to receive contents as yet unknown. Whiffs of thoughts relating to the business in hand, to the car I had recently acquired, to this or that feature of the surrounding country, played, as it were, on the outside of my mind, and if anything did echo in my vast inward wilderness it was merely the dim sensation of some force driving me along.

A clever Lett whom I used to know in Moscow in 1919 said to me once that the clouds of brooding which occasionally and without any reason came over me were a sure sign of my ending in a madhouse. He was exaggerating, of course; during this last year I have thoroughly tested the remarkable qualities of clarity and cohesion exhibited by the logical masonry in which my strongly developed, but perfectly normal mind indulged. Frolics of the intuition, artistic vision, inspiration, all the grand things which have lent my life such beauty, may, I expect, strike the layman, clever though he be, as the preface of mild lunacy. But don't you worry; my health is perfect, my body both clean within and without, my gait easy; I neither drink nor smoke excessively, nor do I live in riot. Thus, in the pink of health, well dressed and young-looking, I roved the countryside described above; and the secret inspiration did not deceive me. I did find the thing that I had been unconsciously tracking. Let me repeat—incredible! I was gazing at a marvel, and its perfection, its lack of cause and object filled me with a strange awe. But perhaps already then, while I gazed, my reason had begun to probe the perfection, to search for the cause, to guess at the object.

He drew his breath in with a sharp sniff; his face broke into ripples of life—this slightly marred the marvel, but still it was there. He then opened his eyes, blinked at me askance, sat up, and with endless yawns—could not get his fill of them —started scratching his scalp, both hands deep in his brown greasy hair.

He was a man of my age, lank, dirty, with a three days' stubble on his chin; there was a narrow glimpse of pink flesh between the lower edge of his collar (soft, with two round slits meant for an absent pin) and the upper end of his shirt. His thin-knitted tie dangled sideways, and there was not a button to his shirt front. A few pale violets were fading in his buttonhole; one of them had got loose and hung head downward. Near him lay a shabby knapsack; an opened flap revealed a pretzel and the greater part of a sausage with the usual connotations of ill-timed lust and brutal amputation. I sat examining the tramp with astonishment; he seemed to have donned that gawky disguise for an old-fashioned slumkin-lumpkin fancy dress ball.

"I could do with a smoke," said he in Czech. His voice turned out to be unexpectedly low-tuned, even sedate, and with two forked fingers he made the gesture of holding a cigarette. I thrust toward him my large cigarette case; my eyes did not once leave his face. He bent a little nearer, pressing his hand against the earth as he did so, and I took the opportunity of inspecting his ear and hollow temple.

"German ones," said he and smiled—showed his gums. This disappointed me, but happily his smile vanished immediately. (By this time I was loath to part with the marvel.)

"German yourself?" he inquired in that language, his fingers twirling and pressing the cigarette. I said Yes and clicked my lighter under his nose. He greedily joined his hands roofwise above the trembling flame. Blue-black, square fingernails.

"I'm German, too," said he, puffing smoke. "That is, my father was German, but my mother was Czech, came from Pilsen."

I kept expecting from him an outburst of surprise, great laughter perhaps, but he remained impassive. Only then did I realize what an oaf he was.

"Slept like a top," said he to himself in a tone of fatuous complacency, and spat with gusto.

"Out of work?" I asked.

Mournfully he nodded several times and spat again. It is always a wonder to me the amount of saliva that simple folk seem to possess.

"I can walk more than my boots can," said he looking at his feet. Indeed, he was sadly shod.

He rolled slowly onto his belly and, as he surveyed the distant gasworks and a skylark that soared up from a furrow, he went on musingly:

"That was a good job I had last year in Saxony, not far from the frontier. Gardening. Best thing in the world! Later on I worked in a pastry shop. Every night after work, me and my friend used to cross the frontier for a pint of beer. Seven miles there and as many back. The Czech beer was cheaper than ours and the wenches fatter. There was a time, too, when I played the fiddle and kept a white mouse."

Now let us glance from the side, but just in passing, without any physiognomizing; not too closely, please, gentlemen, or you might get the shock of your lives. Or perhaps you might not. Alas, after all that has happened I have come to know the partiality and fallaciousness of human eyesight. Anyhow, here is the picture: two men reclining on a patch of sickly grass; one, a smartly dressed fellow, slashing his knee with a yellow glove; the other, a vague-eyed vagabond, lying full length and voicing his grievances against life. Crisp rustle of neighboring thornbush. Flying clouds. A windy day in May with little shivers like those that run along the coat of a horse. Rattle of a motor lorry from the highroad. A lark's small voice in the sky.

The tramp had lapsed into silence; then spoke again, pausing to expectorate. One thing and another. On and on. Sighed sadly. Lying prone, bent his legs back till the calves touched his bottom, and then again stretched them out.

"Look here, you," I blurted. "Don't you really *see* anything?"

He rolled over and sat up.

"What's the idea?" he asked, a frown of suspicion darkening his face.

I said: "You must be blind."

For some ten seconds we kept looking into each other's eyes. Slowly I raised my right arm, but his left did not rise, as I had almost expected it to do. I closed my left eye, but both his eyes remained open. I showed him my tongue. He muttered again:

"What's up? What's up?"

I produced a pocket mirror. Even as he took it, he pawed

at his face, then glanced at his palm, but found neither blood nor bird spat. He looked at himself in the sky-blue glass. Gave it back to me with a shrug.

"You fool," I cried. "Don't you see that we two—don't you see, you fool, that we are— Now listen—take a good look at me...."

I drew his head sideways to mine, so that our temples touched; in the glass two pairs of eyes danced and swam.

When he spoke his tone was condescending:

"A rich man never quite resembles a poor one, but I dare say you know better. Now I remember once seeing a pair of twins at a fair, in August 1926—or was it September? Now let me see. No. August. Well, that was really some likeness. Nobody could tell the one from the other. You were promised a hundred marks if you spotted the least difference. 'All right,' says Fritz (Big Carrot, we called him) and lands one twin a wallop on the ear. 'There you are,' he says, 'one of them has a red ear, and the other hasn't, so just hand over the money if you don't mind.' What a laugh we had!"

His eyes sped over the dove-grey cloth of my suit; slid down the sleeve; tripped and pulled up at the gold watch on my wrist.

"Couldn't you find some work for me?" he asked, cocking his head.

Note: it was he and not I who first perceived the masonic bond in our resemblance; and as the resemblance itself had been established by me, I stood toward him—according to his subconscious calculation—in a subtle state of dependence, as if I were the mimic and he the model. Naturally, one always prefers people to say: "He resembles you," and not the other way round. In appealing to me for help this petty scoundrel was just feeling the ground in view of future demands. At the back of his muddled brain there lurked, maybe, the reflection that I ought to be thankful to him for his generously granting me, by the mere fact of his own existence, the occasion of looking like him. Our resemblance struck me as a freak bordering on the miraculous. What interested him was mainly my wishing to see any resemblance at all. He appeared to my eyes as my double, that is, as a creature bodily identical with me. It was this absolute sameness which gave me so piercing a thrill. He on his part saw in me a doubtful imitator. I wish to lay stress, however, on the dimness of those ideas of his. He would certainly not have understood my comments upon them, the dullard.

"I am afraid there is not much I can do for you at the moment," I answered coldly. "But leave me your address."

I took out my notebook and silver pencil.

He smiled ruefully: "No good saying I live in a villa; better to sleep in a hayloft than on moss in a wood, but better to sleep on moss than on a hard bench."

"Still, I should like to know where to find you."

He thought this over and then said: "This autumn I am sure to be at the same village where I worked last year. You might send a line to the post office there. It is not far from Tarnitz. Here, let me write it down for you."

His name turned out to be Felix, "the happy one." What his surname was, gentle reader, is no business of yours. His awkward handwriting seemed to creak at every turning. He wrote with his left hand. It was time for me to go. I put ten crowns into cap. With a condescending grin he offered his hand, hardly bothering to sit up. I grasped it only because it provided me with the curious sensation of Narcissus fooling Nemesis by helping his image out of the brook.

Then almost at a run I returned the way I had come. When

I looked over my shoulder I saw his dark lank figure among
the bushes. He was lying supine, his legs crossed in the air
and his arms under his head.

Suddenly I felt limp, dizzy, dead-tired, as after some long
and disgusting orgy. The reason for this sickly-sweet after-
glow was that he had, with a cool show of absent-minded-
ness, pocketed my silver pencil. A procession of silver pencils
marched down an endless tunnel of corruption. As I followed
the edge of the road I now and then closed my eyes till I all
but tumbled into the ditch. Then afterwards, at the office,
in the course of a business conversation, I simply craved to
tell my interlocutor: "Queer thing has just happened to me!
Now you would hardly believe . . ." But I said nothing, thus
setting a precedent for secrecy.

When at last I got back to my hotel room, I found there,
amid mercurial shadows and framed in frizzly bronze, Felix
awaiting me. Pale-faced and solemn he drew near. He was
now well-shaven; his hair was smoothly brushed back. He
wore a dove-grey suit with a lilac tie. I took out my handkerchief; he took out his handkerchief too. A truce, parleying.

Some of the countryside had got into my nostrils. I blew
my nose and sat down on the edge of the bed, continuing the
while to consult the mirror. I remember that the small
marks of conscious existence such as the dust in my nose, the
black dirt between the heel and the shank of one shoe, hun-
ger, and presently the rough brown taste tinged with lemon
of a large flat veal cutlet in the grillroom, strangely absorbed
my attention as if I were looking for, and finding (and still
doubting a little) proofs that I was I, and that this I (a second-
rate businessman with ideas) was really at a hotel, dining,
reflecting on business matters, and had nothing in common
with a certain tramp who, at the moment, was lolling under

a bush. And then again, the thrill of that marvel made my heart miss a beat. That man, especially when he slept, when his features were motionless, showed me my own face, my mask, the flawlessly pure image of my corpse—I use the latter term merely because I wish to express with the utmost clarity —express what? Namely this: that we had identical features, and that, in a state of perfect repose, this resemblance was strikingly evident, and what is death, if not a face at peace— its artistic perfection? Life only marred my double; thus a breeze dims the bliss of Narcissus; thus, in the painter's absence, there comes his pupil and by the superfluous flush of unbidden tints disfigures the portrait painted by the master.

And then, thought I, was not I, who knew and liked my own face, in a better position than others to notice my double, for it is not everyone who is so observant; and it often happens that people comment upon the striking resemblance between two persons, who, though acquainted, do not suspect their own likeness (and who start denying it hotly if told). All the same, I had never before supposed it possible that there could exist such perfect resemblance as that between Felix and me. I have seen brothers resembling each other, twins. On the screen I have seen a man meeting his double; or better to say an actor playing two parts with, as in our case, the difference of social standing naïvely stressed, so that in one part he was a slinking rough, and in the other a staid *bourgeois* in a car—as if, really, a pair of identical tramps, or a pair of identical gents, would have been less fun. Yes, I have seen all that, but the likeness between twin brothers is spoiled like an equiradical rhyme by the stamp of kinship, while a film actor in a double part can hardly deceive anyone, for even if he does appear in both impersonations at once, the eye cannot help tracing a line down the middle where the halves of the picture have been joined.

Our case, however, was neither that of identical twins (sharing blood meant for one) nor of a stagewizard's trickery.

How I long to convince you! And I will, I will convince you! I will force you all, you rogues, to believe ... though I am afraid that words alone, owing to their special nature, are unable to convey visually a likeness of that kind: the two faces should be pictured side by side, by means of real colors, not words, then and only then would the spectator see my point. An author's fondest dream is to turn the reader into a spectator; is this ever attained? The pale organisms of literary heroes feeding under the author's supervision swell gradually with the reader's lifeblood; so that the genius of a writer consists in giving them the faculty to adapt themselves to that —not very appetizing—food and thrive on it, sometimes for centuries. But at the present moment it is not literary methods that I need, but the plain, crude obviousness of the painter's art.

Look, this is my nose; a big one of the northern type, with a hard bone somewhat arched and the fleshy part tipped up and almost rectangular. And that is his nose, a perfect replica of mine. Here are the two sharply drawn furrows on both sides of my mouth with lips so thin as to seem licked away. He has got them, too. Here are the cheekbones—but this is a passport list of facial features meaning nothing; an absurd convention. Somebody told me once that I looked like Amundsen, the Polar explorer. Well, Felix, too, looked like Amundsen. But it is not every person that can recall Amundsen's face. I myself recall it but faintly, nor am I sure whether there had not been some mix-up with Nansen. No, I can explain nothing.

Simpering, that is what I am. Well do I know that I have proved my point. Going on splendidly. You now see both of us, reader. Two, but with a single face. You must not suppose, however, that I am ashamed of possible slips and type errors in the book of nature. Look nearer: I possess large yellowish teeth; his are whiter and set more closely together, but is that really important? On my forehead a vein stands out like a capital M imperfectly drawn, but when I sleep my brow is as smooth as that of my double. And those ears . . . the convolutions of his are but very slightly altered in comparison with mine: here more compressed, there smoothed out. We have eyes of the same shape, narrowly slit with sparse lashes, but his iris is paler than mine.

This was about all in the way of distinctive markings that I discerned at that first meeting. During the following night my rational memory did not cease examining such minute flaws, whereas with the irrational memory of my senses I kept seeing, despite everything, myself, my own self, in the sorry disguise of a tramp, his face motionless, with chin and cheeks bristle-shaded, as happens to a dead man overnight.

Why did I tarry in Prague? I had finished my business. I was free to return to Berlin. Why did I go back to those slopes next morning, to that road? I had no trouble in finding the exact spot where he had sprawled the day before. I discovered there a golden cigarette-end, a dead violet, a scrap of Czech newspaper, and—that pathetically impersonal trace which the unsophisticated wanderer is wont to leave under a bush: one large, straight, manly piece and a thinner one coiled over it. Several emerald flies completed the picture. Whither had he gone? Where had he passed the night? Empty riddles. Somehow I felt horribly uncomfortable in a vague heavy way, as if the whole experience had been an evil deed.

I returned to the hotel for my suitcase and hurried to the station. There, at the entrance to the platform, were two rows of nice low benches with backs carved and curved in perfect accordance with the human spine. Some people were sitting there; a few were dozing. It occurred to me that I should suddenly see him there, fast asleep, hands open and one last violet still in his buttonhole. People would notice us together; jump up, surround us, drag us to the police station ... why? Why do I write this? Just the usual rush of my pen? Or is it indeed a crime in itself for two people to be as alike as two drops of blood?

# Chapter Two

I have grown much too used to an outside view of myself, to being both painter and model, so no wonder my style is denied the blessed grace of spontaneity. Try as I may I do not succeed in getting back into my original envelope, let alone making myself comfortable in my old self; the disorder there is far too great; things have been moved, the lamp is black and dead, bits of my past litter the floor.

Quite a happy past, I dare say. I owned in Berlin a small but attractive flat, three and a half rooms, sunny balcony, hot water, central heating; Lydia, my thirty-year-old wife, and Elsie, our seventeen-year-old maid. Close at hand was the garage where stood that delightful little car—a dark-blue two-seater, paid for in installments. On the balcony, a bulging round-headed hoary cactus grew bravely though slowly. I got my tobacco always at the same shop, and was greeted there by a radiant smile. A similar smile welcomed my wife at the store which supplied us with eggs and butter. On Saturday nights we went to a café or to the pictures. We belonged to the cream of the smug middle class, or so it would seem. I did not, however, upon coming home from office, take off my shoes to lie down on the couch with the evening paper. Nor did conversation with my wife consist solely of smallish numerals. Nor again did my thoughts always stick to the adventures of the chocolate I made. I may even confess that certain Bohemian tastes were not entirely foreign to my nature.

As to my attitude toward new Russia, let me declare straightaway that I did not share my wife's views. Coming from her painted lips, the term "Bolshevik" acquired a note of habitual and trivial hatred—no, "hatred" is, I am afraid, too strong a word here. It was something homely, elementary, womanish, for she disliked Bolsheviks as one dislikes rain (on Sundays especially) or bedbugs (especially in new lodgings), and Bolshevism meant to her a nuisance akin to the common cold. She took it for granted that facts confirmed her opinion; their truth was too obvious to be discussed. Bolsheviks did not believe in God; that was naughty of them, but what else could one expect from sadists and hooligans?

When I used to say that Communism in the long run was a great and necessary thing; that young, new Russia was producing wonderful values, although unintelligible to Western minds and unacceptable to destitute and embittered exiles; that history had never yet known such enthusiasm, asceticism, and unselfishness, such faith in the impending sameness of us all—when I used to talk like this, my wife would answer serenely: "I think you are saying it to tease me, and I think it's not kind." But really I was quite serious for I have always believed that the mottled tangle of our elusive lives demands such essential change; that Communism shall indeed create a beautifully square world of identical brawny fellows, broad-shouldered and microcephalous; and that a hostile attitude toward it is both childish and preconceived, reminding me of the face my wife makes—nostrils strained and one eyebrow lifted (the childish and preconceived idea of a vamp) every time she catches sight of herself in the mirror.

Now that is a word I loathe, the ghastly thing! I have had none of the article ever since I stopped shaving. Anyway, the mere mention of it has just given me a nasty shock, broken the flow of my story (please imagine what should follow here —the history of mirrors); then, too, there are crooked ones, monsters among mirrors: a neck bared, no matter how slightly, draws out suddenly into a downward yawn of flesh, to meet which there stretches up from below the belt another marchpane-pink nudity and both merge into one; a crooked mirror strips its man or starts to squash him, and lo! there is produced a man-bull, a man-toad, under the pressure of countless glass atmospheres; or else, one is pulled out like dough and then torn into two.

Enough—let us get on—roars of laughter are not in my line! Enough, it is not all so simple as you seem to think, you swine, you! Oh, yes, I am going to curse at you, none can forbid me to curse. And not to have a looking glass in my room—that is also my right! True, even in the event of my being confronted by one (bosh, what have I to fear?) it would reflect a bearded stranger—for that beard of mine has done jolly well, and in such a short time too! I am disguised so perfectly, as to be invisible to my own self. Hair comes sprouting out of every pore. There must have been a tremendous stock of shag inside me. I hide in the natural jungle that has grown out of me. There is nothing to fear. Silly superstition!

See here, I am going to write that word again. Mirror. Mirror. Well, has anything happened? Mirror, mirror, mirror. As many times as you like—I fear nothing. A mirror. To catch sight of oneself in a mirror. I was referring to my wife when speaking of that. Difficult to talk if one is constantly interrupted.

By the way she, too, was given to superstition. The "touchwood" fad. Hurriedly, with an air of decision, her lips compressed, she would glance about for some bare, unpolished timber, find only the underside of a table, then touch it with her stumpy fingers (little cushions of flesh round the strawberry-bright nails which, though lacquered, were never quite clean; the nails of a child)—touch it quickly whilst the mention of happiness still hung warm in the air. She believed in dreams: to dream you had lost a tooth portended the death of someone you knew; and if there came blood with the tooth, then it would be the death of a relative. A field of daisies foretold meeting again one's first lover. Pearls stood for tears. It was very bad to see oneself all in white sitting at the head of the table. Mud meant money; a cat—treason; the sea—trouble for the soul. She was fond of recounting her dreams, circumstantially and at length. Alas! I am writing of her in the past tense. Let me brace up the buckle of my story one hole tighter.

She hates Lloyd George; had it not been for him, the Russian Empire would not have fallen; and—generally: "I could strangle those English with my own hands." Germans get their due for that sealed train in which Bolshevism was tinned, and Lenin imported to Russia. Speaking of the French: "Do you know, Ardalion [a cousin of hers who had fought with the White Army] says they behaved like downright cads in Odessa during the evacuation." At the same time she considers the English type of face to be (after mine) the handsomest on earth; respects Germans because they are musical and steady; and declares she adores Paris, where we once happened to spend a few days. These opinions of hers stand as stiff as statues in their niches. On the contrary, her position in respect to the Russian folk has, on the whole, undergone a certain evolution. In 1920 she was still saying: "The genuine Russian peasant is a monarchist"; now she says: "The genuine Russian peasant is extinct."

She is little educated and little observant. We discovered one day that to her the term "mystic" was somehow dimly connected with "mist" and "mistake" and "stick," but that she had not the least idea what a mystic really was. The only kind of tree she is capable of identifying is the birch: reminds her of her native woodland, she says.

She is a great gobbler of books, but reads only trash, memorizing nothing and leaving out the longer descriptions. She goes for her books to a Russian library; there she seats herself down and is a long time choosing; fumbles at books on the table; takes one, turns its pages, peers into it sideways, like an investigative hen; puts it away, takes up another, opens it—all of which is performed on the table's surface and with the help of one hand only; she notices that she has opened the book upside down, whereupon it is given a turn of ninety degrees—not more, for she discards it to make a dash at the volume which the librarian is about to offer to another lady; the whole process lasts more than an hour, and I do not know what prompts her final selection. Perhaps the title.

Once I brought back from a railway journey some rotten detective novel with a crimson spider amid a black web on its cover. She dipped into it and found it terribly thrilling—felt that she simply could not help taking a peep at the end, but as that would spoil everything, she shut her eyes tight and tore the book in two down its back and hid the second, concluding, portion; then, later, she forgot the place and was a long, long time searching the house for the criminal she herself had concealed, repeating the while in a small voice: "It was so exciting, so terribly exciting; I know I shall die if I don't find out——"

She has found out now. Those pages that explained everything were securely hidden; still, they were found—all of them except one, perhaps. Indeed, a lot of things have happened; now duly explained. Also that came to pass which she feared most. Of all omens it was the weirdest. A shattered mirror. Yes, it did happen, although not quite in the ordinary way. The poor dead woman.

Tum-tee-tum. And once more—TUM! No, I have not gone mad. I am merely producing gleeful little sounds. The kind of glee one experiences upon making an April fool of someone. And a damned good fool I *have* made of someone. Who is he? Gentle reader, look at yourself in the mirror, as you seem to like mirrors so much.

And now, all of a sudden I feel sad—the real thing, this time. I have just visualized, with shocking vividness, that cactus on the balcony, those blue rooms, that flat of ours in one of those newfangled houses built in the modern boxlike, space-cheating, let-us-have-no-nonsense style. And there, in my world of neatness and cleanliness, the disorder Lydia spread, the sweet vulgar tang of her perfume. But her faults, her innocent dullness, her school-dormitory habit of having the giggles in bed, did not really annoy me. We never quarreled, never did I make a single complaint to her—no matter what piffle she spouted in public, or how tastelessly she dressed. She was anything but good at distinguishing shades, poor soul. She thought it just right if the main colors matched, this satisfying thoroughly her sense of tone, and so she would flaunt a hat of grass-green felt with an olive-green or eau de Nil dress. She liked everything "to be echoed." If, for instance, the sash was black, then she found it absolutely necessary to have some little black fringe or little black frill about her throat. In the first years of our married life she used to wear linen with Swiss embroidery. She was perfectly capable of putting on a wispy frock together with thick autumn shoes; no, decidedly, she had not the faintest notion of the mysteries of harmony, and this was connected with her being wretchedly untidy. Her slovenliness showed in the very way she walked, for she had a knack of treading her left shoe down at heel.

It made me shudder to glance into her chest of drawers where there writhed higgledy-piggledy a farrago of rags, ribbons, bits of silk, her passport, a wilted tulip, some pieces of moth-eaten fur, sundry anachronisms (gaiters for example, as worn by girls ages ago) and suchlike impossible rubbish. Quite often, too, there would dribble into the cosmos of my beautifully arranged things some tiny and very dirty lace handkerchief or a solitary stocking, torn. Stockings seemed positively to burn on those brisk calves of hers.

Not a jot did she understand of household matters. Her receptions were dreadful. There would always be, in a little dish, broken bars of milk chocolate as offered in poor provincial families. I sometimes used to ask myself, what on earth did I love her for? Maybe for the warm hazel iris of her fluffy eyes, or for the natural side-wave of her brown hair, done anyhow, or again for that movement of her plump shoulders. But probably the truth was that I loved her because she loved me. To her I was the ideal man: brains, pluck. And there was none dressed better. I remember, once, when I first put on that new dinner jacket, with the vast trousers, she clasped her hands, sank down on a chair and murmured:

"Oh, Hermann. . . ." It was ravishment bordering upon something like heavenly woe.

With, perhaps, the ill-defined feeling that by further embellishing the image of the man she loved, I was meeting her halfway, and doing her and her happiness a good turn, I took advantage of her confidence and during the ten years we lived together told her such a heap of lies about myself, my past, my adventures, that it would have been beyond my powers to hold it all in my head, always ready for reference. But she used to forget everything. Her umbrella stayed with all our acquaintances in turn; her lipstick turned up in incomprehensible places such as her cousin's shirtpocket; the thing she had read in the morning paper would be told me at night somewhat as follows: "Let me see, where did I read it, and *what was* it exactly? . . . I just had it by the tail—oh, please, do help me!" Giving her a letter to post was equal to throwing it into the river, leaving the rest to the acumen of the stream and the recipient's piscatorial leisure.

She mixed dates, names, faces. After having invented something I never returned to it; she soon forgot, the story sank to the bottom of her consciousness, but there remained on the surface the ever-renewed rings of humble wonder. Her love almost crossed the boundary limiting all the rest of her feelings. On certain nights, when June and moon rhymed, her most settled thoughts turned into timid nomads. It did not last, they did not wander far, the world was locked again; and a very simple world it was, with the greatest complication in it amounting to a search for the telephone number which she had jotted down on one of the pages of a library book, borrowed by the very person whom she wished to ring up.

She was plump, short, rather formless, but then pudgy

women alone rouse me. I simply have no use for the long
young lady, the scrawny flapper, the proud smart whore who
struts up and down Tauentzienstrasse in her shiny tight-
laced boots. Not only had I always been eminently satisfied
with my meek bedmate and her cherubic charms, but I had
noticed lately, with gratitude to nature and a thrill of surprise, that the violence and the sweetness of my nightly joys
were being raised to an exquisite vertex owing to a certain
aberration which, I understand, is not as uncommon as I
thought at first among high-strung men in their middle
thirties. I am referring to a well-known kind of "dissociation." With me it started in fragmentary fashion a few months
before my trip to Prague. For example, I would be in bed
with Lydia, winding up the brief series of preparatory caresses
she was supposed to be entitled to, when all at once I would
become aware that imp Split had taken over. My face was
buried in the folds of her neck, her legs had started to clamp
me, the ashtray toppled off the bed table, the universe followed—but at the same time, incomprehensibly and delightfully, I was standing naked in the middle of the room, one
hand resting on the back of the chair where she had left her
stockings and panties. The sensation of being in two places
at once gave me an extraordinary kick; but this was nothing
compared to later developments. In my impatience to split
I would bundle Lydia to bed as soon as we had finished
supper. The dissociation had now reached its perfect phase.
I sat in an armchair half a dozen paces away from the bed
upon which Lydia had been properly placed and distributed.
From my magical point of vantage I watched the ripples
running and plunging along my muscular back, in the labora-
torial light of a strong bed-lamp that picked out a mother-
of-pearl glint in the pink of her knees and a bronze gleam

in her hair spread on the pillow—which were about the only bits of her I could see while that big back of mine had not yet slid off to prop up again its panting front half in the audience. The next phase came when I realized that the greater the interval between my two selves the more I was ecstasied; therefore I used to sit every night a few inches farther from the bed, and soon the back legs of my chair reached the threshold of the open door. Eventually I found myself sitting in the parlor—while making love in the bedroom. It was not enough. I longed to discover some means to remove myself at least a hundred yards from the lighted stage where I performed; I longed to contemplate that bedroom scene from some remote upper gallery in a blue mist under the swimming allegories of the starry vault; to watch a small but distinct and very active couple through opera glasses, field glasses, a tremendous telescope, or optical instruments of yet unknown power that would grow larger in proportion to my increasing rapture. Actually, I never got farther back than the console in the parlor, and even so found my view of the bed cut off by the doorjamb unless I opened the wardrobe in the bedroom to have the bed reflected in the oblique speculum or *spiegel*. Alas, one April night, with the harps of rain aphrodisiacally burbling in the orchestra, as I was sitting at my maximum distance of fifteen rows of seats and looking forward to an especially good show—which, indeed, had already started, with my acting self in colossal form and most inventive—from the distant bed, where I thought I was, came Lydia's yawn and voice stupidly saying that if I were not yet coming to bed, I might bring her the red book she had left in the parlor. It lay, in fact, on the console near my chair, and rather than bring it I threw it bedward with a windmill flapping of pages. This strange and awful jolt broke the spell.

I was like an insular species of bird that has lost the knack of rising into the air and, like the penguin, flies only in its sleep. I tried hard to recapture the split, and perhaps would have at last succeeded, had not a new and wonderful obsession obliterated in me all desire to resume those amusing but rather banal experiments.

Otherwise, my connubial bliss was complete. She loved me without reservations, without retrospection; her devotion seemed part of her nature. I do not know why I have lapsed again into the past tense; but never mind, my pen finds it more convenient so. Yes, she loved me, loved me faithfully. She liked to examine my face this way and that; with finger and thumb, compasswise, she measured my features: the some-what prickly area above the upper lip, with the longish groove down the middle; the spacious forehead with its twin swell-ings above the brows; and the nail of her index finger would follow the lines on both sides of my mouth, which was always shut tight and insensitive to tickling. A big face and none too simple; modeled by special order; with a gloss on the cheek-bones, the cheeks themselves slightly hollowed and, on the second shaveless day, overspread with a brigandish growth, reddish in certain lights, exactly the same as his beard. Our eyes alone were not quite identical but what likeness did exist between them was a mere luxury; for his were closed as he lay on the ground before me, and though I have never really seen, only felt, my eyelids when shut, I know that they dif-fered in nothing from his eye-eaves—a good word, that! Ornate, but good, and a welcome guest to my prose. No, I am not getting in the least excited; my self-control is perfect. If every now and again my face pops out, as from behind a hedge, perhaps to the prim reader's annoyance, it is really for the latter's good: let him get used to my countenance;

and in the meantime I shall be chuckling quietly over his not knowing whether it was my face or that of Felix. Here I am! and now—gone again; or may be it was not I! Only by this method can I hope to teach the reader a lesson, demonstrating to him that ours was not an imaginary resemblance, but a real possibility, even more—a real fact, yes, a fact, however fanciful and absurd it might seem.

On coming back from Prague to Berlin, I found Lydia in the kitchen engaged in beating an egg in a glass—"gogglemoggle," we called it. "Throaty aches," she said in a childish voice; then put down the glass upon the edge of the stove, wiped her yellow lips with the back of her wrist and proceeded to kiss my hand. She had on a pink frock, pinkish stockings, dilapidated slippers. The evening sun checkered the kitchen. Again she started to turn the spoon in the thick yellow stuff, grains of sugar crunched slightly, it was still clammy, the spoon did not move smoothly with the velvety ovality that was required. On the stove lay open a battered book. There was a note scribbled in the margin by some person unknown, with a blunt pencil: "Sad, but true" followed by three exclamation marks with their respective dots skidding. I perused the phrase that had appealed so much to one of my wife's predecessors: "Love thy neighbor," said Sir Reginald, "is nowadays not quoted on the stock exchange of human relations."

"Well—had a good trip?" asked Lydia as she went on energetically turning the handle, with the box-part held firm between her knees. The coffee beans crackled, richly odorous; the mill was still working with a rumbling and creaking effort; then came an easing, a yielding; gone all resistance; empty.

I have got muddled somehow. As in a dream. She was making that goggle-moggle—not coffee.

"Could have been worse," I said, referring to the trip. "And you, how are you getting on?"

Why did I not tell her of my incredible adventure? I, who would fake wonders for her by the million, seemed not to dare, with those polluted lips of mine, tell her of a wonder that was real. Or maybe something else withheld me. An author does not show people his first draft; a child in the womb is not referred to as Tiny Tom or Belle; a savage refrains from naming objects of mysterious import and uncertain temper; Lydia herself disliked my reading a book she had not yet finished.

For several days I remained oppressed by that meeting. It oddly disturbed me to think that all the time my double was trudging along roads unknown to me, and that he was underfed and cold and wet—and perhaps had caught a chill. I longed for him to find work: it would have been sweeter to know that he were snug and warm—or at least safe in prison. All the same it was not at all my intention to undertake any such measures as might improve his circumstances. I was not in the least keen to pay for his upkeep, and it would have been impossible to find him a job in Berlin, swarming as it was with ragamuffins. Indeed, to be quite frank, I found it somehow preferable to hold him at a certain distance from me as though any proximity would have broken the spell of our likeness. From time to time I might send him a little money lest he should slip and perish in the course of his far wanderings and thus cease to be my faithful representative, a live circulating copy of my face. . . . Kind but idle thoughts, for the man had no permanent address. So let us tarry (thought I) until, on a certain autumn day, he calls at that village post office somewhere in Saxony.

May passed, and in my mind the memory of Felix healed up. I note for my own pleasure the smooth run of that sentence: the banal narratory tone of the first two words, and then that long sigh of imbecile contentment. Sensation lovers, however, might be interested to observe that, generally speaking, the term "heal up" is employed only when alluding to wounds. But this is only mentioned in passing; no harm meant. Now there is something else I should like to note—namely, that writing with me has become an easier matter: my tale has gained impetus. I have now boarded that bus (mentioned at the beginning), and, what is more, I have a comfortable window seat. And thus, too, I used to drive to my office, before I acquired the car.

That summer it had to work pretty hard, the shiny blue little Icarus. Yes, I was quite taken by my new toy. Lydia and I would often buzz away for the whole day to the country. We always took with us that cousin of hers called Ardalion, who was a painter: a cheery soul, but a rotten painter. By all accounts he was as poor as a sparrow. If people did have their portraits done by him, it was sheer charity on their part, or weakness of character (the man could be hideously insistent). From me, and probably also from Lydia, he used to borrow small cash; and of course he contrived to stay for dinner. He was always behind with his rent, and when he did pay it, he paid it in kind. In still life to be precise . . . square apples on a slanting cloth, or phallic tulips in a leaning vase. All this his landlady would frame at her own cost, so that her dining room made one think of an avant-garde, Philistine exhibition. He fed at a little Russian restaurant which, he said, he had once "slapped up" (meaning that he had decorated its walls); he used an even richer expression, for he hailed from Moscow, where people are fond of waggish slang full of lush trivialities (I shall not attempt to render it). The funny part was, that in spite of his poverty, he had somehow managed to purchase a piece of ground, a three hours' drive from Berlin—that is, he had somehow managed to make a down payment of a hundred marks, and did not bother about the rest; in fact, never meant to disgorge another penny, as he considered that the land, fertilized by his first payment, was henceforth his own till doomsday. It measured, that land, about two and a half tennis courts in length, and abutted on a rather beautiful little lake. A Y-stemmed couple of insep-arable birches grew there (or a couple of couples, if you counted their reflections); also several black-alder bushes; a little farther off stood five pine trees and still farther inland one came upon a patch of heather, courtesy of the surround-ing wood. The ground was not fenced—there had not been money enough for that. I strongly suspected Ardalion of wait-ing for the two adjacent allotments to get fenced first, which would automatically legitimate the boundaries of his prop-erty and give him an enclosure gratis; but the neighboring bits were still unsold. On the shores of that lake business was slack, the place being damp, mosquito infested, and far from the village; then also there was no road connecting it with the highway, and nobody knew when that road would be made.

It was, I remember, on a Sunday morning in mid-June that, yielding to Ardalion's rapturous persuasions, we went there for the first time. On our way we stopped to pick up the fellow. Long did I keep toot-tooting, with my eyes fixed on his window. That window slept soundly. Lydia put her hands to her mouth and cried out in a trumpet voice: "Ar-dally-o-o!" In one of the lower windows, just above the signboard of a pub (which, by its look, somehow suggested that Ardalion owed money there) a curtain was dashed aside furiously and a Bismarck-like worthy in frogged dressing gown glanced out with a real trumpet in his hand.

Leaving Lydia in the car, which by now had stopped throbbing, I went up to arouse Ardalion. I found him asleep. He slept in his one-piece bathing suit. Rolling out of bed, he proceeded with silent rapidity to slip on sandals, a blue shirt, and flannel trousers; then he snatched up a briefcase (with a suspicious lump in its cheek) and we went down. A solemn and sleepy expression did not exactly add charm to his fat-nosed face. He was put in the rumble seat.

I did not know the way. He said he knew it as well as he knew his Pater Noster. No sooner had we left Berlin than we went astray. The rest of our drive consisted of making inquiries.

"A glad sight for a landowner!" exclaimed Ardalion, when about noon we passed Koenigsdorf and then sped along the stretch of road he knew. "I shall tell you when to turn. Hail, hail, my ancient trees!"

"Don't play the fool, Ardy dear," said Lydia placidly.

On either side there stretched rough wasteland, the sand-and-heather variety, with a sprinkling of young pines. Then, farther on, the country changed a little; we had now an ordinary field on our right, darkly bordered at some distance by a forest. Ardalion began to fuss anew. On the right-hand side of the highway a bright yellow post grew up and at that spot there branched out at right angles a scarcely discernible road, the ghost of some obsolete road, which presently expired among burdocks and oatgrass.

"This is the turning," said Ardalion grandly and then, with

a sudden grunt, pitched forward into me, for I had put on
the brakes.

You smile, gentle reader? And indeed, why should you not
smile? A pleasant summer day and a peaceful countryside;
a good-natured fool of an artist and a roadside post. . . . That
yellow post. . . . Erected by the man selling the allotments,
sticking up in brilliant solitude, an errant brother of those
other painted posts, which, seventeen kilometers farther
toward the village of Waldau, stood sentinel over more tempt-
ing and expensive acres, that particular landmark subse-
quently became a fixed idea with me. Cut out clearly in
yellow, amid a diffuse landscape, it stood up in my dreams.
By its position my fancies found their bearings. All my
thoughts reverted to it. It shone, a faithful beacon, in the
darkness of my speculations. I have the feeling today that
I *recognized* it, when seeing it for the first time: familiar to
me as a thing of the future. Perhaps I am mistaken; perhaps
the glance I gave it was quite an indifferent one, my sole
concern being not to scrape the mudguard against it while
turning; but all the same, today as I recall it, I cannot sepa-
rate that first acquaintanceship from its mature development.

The road, as already mentioned, lost itself, faded away; the
car creaked crossly, as it bounced on the bumpy ground; I
stopped it and shrugged my shoulders.

Lydia said: "I suggest, Ardy dear, we push on to Waldau
instead; you said there was a large lake there and a café or
something."

"That's out of the question," retorted Ardalion excitedly.
"Firstly, because the café is only just being planned, and
secondly, because I have a lake too. Come on, my dear fellow," he continued, turning to me, "make the old bus move,
you won't be sorry."

In front of us, on higher ground, at a distance of some three hundred feet, a pine forest began. I looked at it and ... well, I can swear that I felt as if I had known it already. Yes, that's it, now I am getting it clear—I certainly did have that queer sensation; it has not been added as an aftertouch. And that yellow post ... How meaningly it looked at me, when I glanced back—as if it were saying: "I am here, I am at your service. ..." And those pines facing me, with their bark resembling reddish snakeskin drawn on tight, and their green fur which the wind was stroking the wrong way; and that bare birch tree on the forest's edge (now, why did I write "bare"? It was not winter yet, winter was still remote), and the day so balmy and almost cloudless, and the little stammering crickets zealously trying to say something beginning with z. ... Yes, it all meant something—no mistake.

"May I ask, *where* you want me to move? I can't see any road."

"Oh, don't be so particular," said Ardalion. "Go ahead, old son. Why, yes, straight on. There, where you see the break. We can just manage it, and once in the wood, it's quite a short run to my place."

"Hadn't we better get out and walk?" proposed Lydia.

"Right you are," I replied, "nobody would dream of stealing a new car abandoned here."

"Yes, much too risky," she admitted at once, "but couldn't you two go along" (Ardalion groaned), "let him show you his place while I wait for you here and then we can proceed to Waldau and swim in the lake and sit in the café?"

"How beastly of you," said Ardalion with great feeling. "Can't you see that I wanted to welcome you on my own land? There were some nice surprises in store for you. I am now very hurt."

[ 36 ]

I started the car, saying as I did so: "Well, if we smash it you pay for repairs."

The jolts made me jump in my seat, beside me Lydia jumped, behind us Ardalion jumped and kept speaking: "We shall soon (bump) get into the wood (bump) and then (bump-bump) the heather will make it easier (bump)."

We did get in. First of all we stuck in deep sand, the motor roared, the wheels kicked; at last we wrenched ourselves free; then branches came brushing against the car's body, scratching its paint. Some sort of path did finally show itself, now getting smothered in a dry crackle of heather, now emerging again to meander between the close-set trunks.

"More to the right," said Ardalion, "a little more to the right. Well, what d'you say to the smell of the pines? Gorgeous, eh? I told you so. Absolutely gorgeous. You may stop here while I go investigating."

He got out and marched away with, at every step, an inspired waggle of his hindquarters.

"Hey, I'm coming too," cried Lydia, but he was going full sail and presently the dense undergrowth hid him.

The engine clicked a little and was still.

"What a creepy spot," said Lydia. "Really, I'd be afraid to stay here all by myself. One could get robbed, murdered— anything. . . ."

A lonely spot, quite so! The pines soughed gently, snow lay about, with bald patches of soil showing black. What nonsense! How could there be snow in June? Ought to be crossed out, were it not wicked to erase; for the real author is not I, but my impatient memory. Understand it just as you please; it is none of *my* business. And the yellow post had a skullcap of snow too. Thus the future shimmers through the past. But enough, let that summer day be in focus again: spotty sunlight; shadows of branches across the blue car; a pine cone upon the footboard, where some day the most unexpected of objects will stand; a shaving brush.

"Is it Tuesday that they are coming?" asked Lydia.

I replied: "No, Wednesday night."

A silence.

"I do only hope," said my wife, "they don't bring it with them as last time."

"And even if they do . . . Why should you bother?"

A silence. Small blue butterflies settling on thyme.

"I say, Hermann, are you quite certain it was Wednesday night?"

(Is the hidden sense worth disclosing? We were talking of trifles, alluding to some people we knew, to their dog, a vicious little creature, which engaged the attention of all present at parties; Lydia only cared for "large dogs with pedigrees"; pronouncing "pedigrees" made her nostrils quiver.)

"Why doesn't he come back?" she said. "He's sure to have lost himself."

I got out of the car and walked around it. Paint scratched everywhere.

Having nothing better to do, Lydia busied herself with Ardalion's lumpy briefcase: felt it, then opened it. I walked off a few steps (no, no—I cannot recall what it was I was brooding over); surveyed some broken twigs that lay at my feet; then turned back again. Lydia was now sitting on the footboard and whistling gently. We both lit cigarettes. Silence. She had a way of letting out smoke sideways, her mouth awry.

From afar came Ardalion's lusty bawl. A minute later he appeared in a clearing and brandished his arms, beckoning us on. We drove slowly after him, circumnavigating the tree trunks. Ardalion strode in front, his manner resolute and businesslike. Something flashed—the lake.

I have already described his lot. He was unable to show me its exact limits. With great stamping steps he measured the meters, stopped, looked back, half bending the leg supporting his weight; then shook his head and went to find a certain tree stump which marked something or other.

The two enlaced birches looked at themselves in the water; there was some fluff floating on its surface, and the rushes gleamed in the sun. The surprise promised us by Ardalion turned out to be a bottle of vodka, which, however, Lydia had already managed to hide. She laughed and she gamboled, for all the world like a croquet ball in her beige bathing costume with that double, red and blue stripe round the middle. When, after having had her fill of riding on Ardalion's back as he slowly swam about ("Don't pinch me, woman, or down you go!"), after much shrieking and spluttering, she came out of the water, her legs looked decidedly hairy, but soon they got dry, and a little bright bloom was all that showed. Before taking a header Ardalion would cross himself; there was, along his shin, a great ugly scar left by the civil war; from the opening in his repulsively flabby bathing suit the silver cross, of moujik pattern, that he wore next to his skin, kept jumping out when he jumped in.

Lydia dutifully besmeared herself with cold cream and lay down on her back placing herself at the disposal of the sun. A few feet away, Ardalion and I made ourselves comfortable in the shade of his best pine tree. From his sadly shrunken briefcase he produced a sketch-book, pencils; and presently I noticed that he was drawing me.

"You've a tricky face," he said, screwing up his eyes.

"Oh, do show me!" cried Lydia without stirring a limb.

"Head a bit higher," said Ardalion. "Thanks, that will do."

"Oh, do show me," she cried again a minute later.

"You first show me where you've chucked my vodka," muttered Ardalion.

"No fear," she replied. "I won't have you drinking when I'm about."

"The woman is dotty! Now, should you suppose, old man, that she has actually buried it? I intended, as a matter of fact, quaffing the cup of brotherhood with you."

"I'll have you stop drinking altogether," cried Lydia, without lifting her greasy eyelids.

"Damned cheek," said Ardalion.

"Tell me," I asked him, "what makes you say I have a tricky face? Where is the snag?"

"Don't know. Lead doesn't get you. Next time I must try charcoal or oil." He erased something; flicked away the rubber dust with the joints of his fingers; cocked his head.

"Funny, I always thought I had a most ordinary face. Try, perhaps, drawing it in profile?"

"Yes, in profile!" cried Lydia (as before: spread-eagled on the sand).

"Well, I shouldn't exactly call it ordinary. A little higher, please. No, if you ask me, I find there is something distinctly rum about it. All your lines sort of slip from under my pencil, slip and are gone."

"Such faces, then, occur seldom, that's what you mean?"

"Every face is unique," pronounced Ardalion.

"Lord, I'm roasting," moaned Lydia, but did not move.

"Well, now, really—unique! ... Isn't that going too far? Take for instance the definite types of human faces that exist in the world; say, zoological types. There are people with the

features of apes; there is also the rat type, the swine type.
Then take the resemblance to celebrities—Napoleons among
men, Queen Victorias among women. People have told me
I reminded them of Amundsen. I have frequently come across
noses *à la* Leo Tolstoy. Then, too, there is the type of face
that makes you think of some particular picture. Ikon-like
faces, madonnas! And what about the kind of resemblance
due to some fashion of life or profession? . . ."

"You'll say next that all Chinamen are alike. You forget,
my good man, that what the artist perceives is, primarily, the
*difference* between things. It is the vulgar who note their
resemblance. Haven't we heard Lydia exclaim at the talkies:
'Oo! Isn't she just like our maid?' "

"Ardy, dear, don't try to be funny," said Lydia.

"But you must concede," I went on, "that sometimes it is
the resemblance that matters."

"When buying a second candlestick," said Ardalion.

There is really no need to go on taking down our conversation. I longed passionately for the fool to start talking about
doubles, but he simply did not. After a while he put up his
sketch-book. Lydia implored him to show her what he had
done. He said he would if she gave him back his vodka.
She refused and was not shown the sketch. The memory of
that day ends in a sunshiny haze, or else mingles with the
recollections of later trips. For that first one was followed
by many others. I developed a somber and painfully acute
liking for that lone wood with the lake shining in its midst.
Ardalion tried hard to bully me into making me meet the
manager and acquire the piece of land next to his, but I was
firm; and even had I been anxious to buy land, I should have
failed all the same to make up my mind, as my business had

taken a sorry turn that summer and I was fed up with everything: that filthy chocolate of mine was ruining me. But I give you my word, gentlemen, my word of honor: not mercenary greed, not merely that, not merely the desire to improve my position ... It is, however, unnecessary to forestall events.

# Chapter Three

How shall we begin this chapter? I offer several variations to choose from. Number one (readily adopted in novels where the narrative is conducted in the first person by the real or substitute author):

It is fine today, but cold, with the wind's violence unabated; under my window the evergreen foliage rocks and rolls, and the postman on the Pignan road walks backwards, clutching at his cap. My restlessness grows. . . .

The distinctive features of this variation are rather obvious: it is clear, for one thing, that while a man is writing, he is situated in some definite place; he is not simply a kind of spirit, hovering over the page. While he muses and writes, there is something or other going on around him; there is, for instance, this wind, this whirl of dust on the road which I see from my window (now the postman has swerved round and, bent double, still fighting, walks forward). A nice refreshing variation, this number one; it allows a breather and helps to bring in the personal note; thus lending life to the story—especially when the first person is as fictitious as all the rest. Well, that is just the point: a trick of the trade, a poor thing worn to shreds by literary fiction-mongers, does not suit me, for I have become strictly truthful. So we may turn to the second variation which consists of at once letting loose a new character, starting the chapter thus:

Orlovius was displeased.

When he happened to be displeased or worried, or merely ignorant of the right answer, he used to pull at the long lobe of his left ear, fringed with grey down; then he would pull at the long lobe of his right ear too, so as to avoid jealousies, and look at you over his plain, honest spectacles and take his time and then at last answer: "It is heavy to say, but I—"

"Heavy" with him meant "hard," as in German; and there was a Teutonic thickness in the solemn Russian he spoke.

Now this second variation of a chapter's beginning is a popular and sound method—but there is something too polished about it; nor do I think it becoming for shy, mournful Orlovius to fling open, spryly, the gates of a new chapter. I submit to your attention my third variation.

In the meantime . . . (the inviting gesture of dots, dots, dots).

Of old, this dodge was the darling of the Kinematograph, *alias* Cinematograph, *alias* Moving Pictures. You saw the hero doing this or that, and in the meantime . . . Dots—and the action switched to the country. In the meantime . . . A new paragraph, please.

. . . Plodding along the sun-parched road and trying to keep in the shade of the apple trees, whenever their crooked whitewashed trunks came marching by its side . . .

No, that is a silly notion: he was not always wandering. Some filthy kulak would require an additional hand; another back would be needed by some beastly miller. Having never been a tramp myself, I failed—and still fail—to rerun his life on my private screen. What I wished to imagine most, was the impression left upon him by a certain morning in May passed on a patch of sickly grass near Prague. He woke up.

At his side a well-dressed gentleman was sitting and staring. Happy thought: might give me a smoke. Turned out to be German. Very insistently (was perhaps not quite right in the head?) kept pressing upon me his pocket mirror; got quite abusive. I gathered it was about likenesses. Well, thought I, let them likenesses be. No concern of mine. Chance of his giving me some easy job. Asked about my address. One can never know, something might come of it.

Later: conversation in a barn on a warm dark night: "Now, as I was saying, that was an odd'un, that bloke I met one day. He made out we were doubles."

A laugh in the darkness: "It was you who saw double, you old sot."

Here another literary device has crept in: the imitation of foreign novels, themselves imitations, which depict the ways of merry vagabonds, good hearty fellows. (My devices seem to have got mixed up a little, I am afraid.)

And speaking of literature, there is not a thing about it that I do not know. It has always been quite a hobby of mine. As a child I composed verse and elaborate stories. I never stole peaches from the hothouse of the North Russian land-owner whose steward my father was. I never buried cats alive. I never twisted the arms of playmates weaker than myself; but, as I say, I composed abstruse verse and elaborate stories, with dreadful finality and without any reason whatever lampooning acquaintances of my family. But I did not write down those stories, neither did I talk about them. Not a day passed without my telling some lie. I lied as a nightingale sings, ecstatically, self-obliviously; reveling in the new life-harmony which I was creating. For such sweet lying my mother would give me a cuff on the ear, and my father thrash me with a riding whip which had once been a bull's sinew. That did not dismay me in the least; rather, on the contrary, it furthered the flight of my fancies. With a stunned ear and burning buttocks, I would lie on my belly among the tall weeds in the orchard, and whistle and dream.

At school I used, invariably, to get the lowest mark for Russian composition, because I had a way of my own with Russian and foreign classics; thus, for example, when rendering "in my own words" the plot of *Othello* (which was, mind you, perfectly familiar to me) I made the Moor skeptical and Desdemona unfaithful.

A sordid bet won from a wenching upperformer resulted in a revolver's coming into my possession; so I would trace with chalk, on the aspen trunks in the wood, ugly, screaming, white faces and proceeded to shoot those wretches, one by one.

I liked, as I like still, to make words look self-conscious and foolish, to bind them by the mock marriage of a pun, to turn them inside out, to come upon them unawares. What is this jest in majesty? This ass in passion? How do God and Devil combine to form a live dog?

For several years I was haunted by a very singular and very nasty dream: I dreamed I was standing in the middle of a long passage with a door at the bottom, and passionately wanting, but not daring to go and open it, and then deciding at last to go, which I accordingly did; but at once awoke with a groan, for what I saw there was unimaginably terrible; to wit, a perfectly empty, newly whitewashed room. That was all, but it was so terrible that I never could hold out; then one night a chair and its slender shadow appeared in the middle of the bare room—not as a first item of furniture but as though somebody had brought it to climb upon it and fix a bit of drapery, and since I knew *whom* I would find there next time stretching up with a hammer and a mouthful of nails, I spat them out and never opened that door again.

At sixteen, while still at school, I began to visit more regularly than before a pleasantly informal bawdy house; after sampling all seven girls, I concentrated my affection on roly-poly Polymnia with whom I used to drink lots of foamy beer at a wet table in an orchard—I simply adore orchards.

During the War, as I may have already mentioned, I moped in a fishing village not far from Astrakhan, and had it not been for books, I doubt whether I should have lived through those dingy years.

I first met Lydia in Moscow (whither I had got by miracle, after wriggling through the accursed hubbub of civil strife), at the flat, belonging to a chance acquaintance of mine, where I lived. He was a Lett, a silent, white-faced man with a cuboidal skull, a crew cut, and fish-cold eyes. By profession a teacher of Latin, he somehow managed, later, to become a prominent Soviet official. Into those lodgings Fate had packed several people who hardly knew one another, and there was among them that other cousin of Lydia's, Ardalion's brother Innocent, who, for some reason or another, got executed by the shooting squad soon after our departure. (To be frank, all this would be far more befitting at the beginning of the first chapter than at the beginning of the third.)

> Bold and scoffing but inwardly tortured
> (O, my soul, will your torch not ignite?),
> From the porch of your God and His orchard
> Why take off for the Earth and the night?

My own, my own! My juvenile experiments in the senseless sounds I loved, hymns inspired by my beery mistress—and "Shvinburne" as he was called in the Baltic provinces... Now, there is one thing I should like to know: was I endowed in those days with any so-called criminal inclinations? Did my adolescence, so dun and dull to all appearances, secrete the possibility of producing a lawbreaker of genius? Or was I, perhaps, only making my way along that ordinary corridor of my dreams, time after time shrieking with horror at finding the room empty, and then one unforgettable day finding it empty no more? Yes, it was then that everything got explained and justified—my longing to open that door, and the queer games I played, and that thirst for falsehood, that addiction to painstaking lying which had seemed so aimless till then. Hermann discovered his alter ego. This happened, as I have had the honor of informing you, on the ninth of May; and in July I visited Orlovius.

The decision, which I had formed and which was now swiftly brought into execution, met with his full approval, the more so, as I was following an old piece of advice of his.

A week later I asked him to dinner. He tucked the corner of his napkin sideways into his collar. While tackling his soup, he expressed displeasure with the trend of political events. Lydia breezily inquired whether there would be any war and with whom? He looked at her over his spectacles, taking his time (such, more or less, was the glimpse you caught of him at the beginning of this chapter) and finally answered: "It is heavy to say, but I think war excluded. When I young was, I came upon the idea of supposing only the best" (he all but turned "best" into "pest," so gross were his lip-consonants). "I hold this idea always. The chief thing by me is optimismus."

"Which comes in very handy, seeing your profession," said I with a smile.

He lowered at me and replied quite seriously:

"But it is pessimismus that gives clients to us."

The end of the dinner was unexpectedly crowned with tea served in glasses. For some unaccountable reason Lydia thought such a finish very clever and nice. Orlovius at any rate was pleased. Ponderously and lugubriously telling us of his old mother, who lived in Dorpat, he held up his glass to stir what remained of his tea in the German fashion—that is, not with a spoon, but by means of a circular motion of the wrist—so as not to waste the sugar settled at the bottom.

The agreement I signed with his firm was, on my part, a curiously hazy and insignificant action. It was about that time I became so depressed, silent, absent-minded; even my unobservant wife noticed a change in me—especially as my lovemaking had lapsed into a drab routine after all that furious dissociation. Once, in the middle of the night (we were lying awake in bed, and the room was impossibly stuffy, notwithstanding the wide-open window), she said:

"You do seem overworked, Hermann; in August we'll go to the seaside."

"Oh," I said, "it's not only that, but town life generally, that's what is boring me to death."

She could not see my face in the dark. After a minute she went on:

"Now, take for instance Aunt Elisa—you know that aunt of mine who lived in France, in Pignan. There *is* such a town as Pignan, isn't there?"

"Yes."

"Well, she doesn't live there any more, but has gone to Nice with the old Frenchman she married. They've got a farm down there."

She yawned.

"My chocolate is going to the devil, old girl," said I and yawned also.

"Everything will be all right," Lydia muttered. "You must have a rest, that's all."

"A change of life, not a rest," said I with the pretense of a sigh.

"Change of life," said Lydia.

"Tell me," I asked her, "wouldn't you like us to live somewhere in a quiet sunny nook, wouldn't it be a treat for you, if I retired from business? The respectable *rentier* sort of thing, eh?"

"I'd like living with you anywhere, Hermann. We'd have Ardalion come too, and perhaps we'd buy a great big dog."

A silence.

"Well, unfortunately we shan't go anywhere. I'm practically broke. That chocolate will have to be liquidated, I suppose."

A belated pedestrian passed by. Chock! And again: chock! He was probably knocking the lamposts with his cane.

"Guess: my first is that sound, my second is an exclamation, my third will be prefixed to me when I'm no more; and my whole is my ruin."

The smooth sizzle of a passing motorcar.

"Well—can't you guess?"

But my fool of a wife was already asleep. I closed my eyes, turned on my side, tried to sleep too; was unsuccessful. Out of the darkness, straight towards me, with jaw protruding and eyes looking straight into mine, came Felix. As he closed up on me he dissolved, and what I saw before me was merely the long, empty road by which he had come. Then again, from afar, there appeared a form, that of a man, giving a knock with his stick to every wayside tree-trunk; nearer and nearer he stalked, and I tried to make out his face. . . . And lo, with jaw protruding and eyes looking straight into mine—

But he faded as before, the moment he reached me, or, better say, he seemed to enter into me, and pass through, as if I were a shadow; and then again there was only the road stretching out expectantly, and again a figure appeared, and again it was he.

I turned on my other side, and for a while all was dark and peaceful, unruffled blackness; then, gradually, a road became perceptible: the same road, but the other way round; and there appeared suddenly before my very face, as if coming out of me, the back of a man's head and the bag strapped to his shoulders; slowly his figure diminished, he was going, going, in another instant would be gone . . . but all of a sudden he stopped, glanced back and retraced his steps, so that his face grew clearer and clearer; and it was my own face.

I turned again, this time lying supine, and then, as if seen through a dark glass, there stretched above me a varnished blue-black sky, a band of sky between the ebon shapes of trees which on either side were slowly receding; but when I lay face downwards, I saw running below me the pebbles and mud of a country road, wisps of dropped hay, a cart rut brimming with rainwater, and in that wind-wrinkled puddle the trembling travesty of my face; which, as I noticed with a shock, was eyeless.

"I always leave the eyes to the last," said Ardalion self-approvingly.

He held before him, at arm's length, the charcoal picture which he had begun making of me, and bent his head this way and that. He used to come frequently, and it was on the balcony that we generally had the sitting. I had plenty of leisure now: it had occurred to me to give myself something in the way of a small holiday.

Lydia was present too, curled up in a wicker armchair

with a book; a half-squashed cigarette end (she never quite crushed them to death) with grim tenacity of life let forth a thin, straight thread of smoke out of the ashtray: now and then some tiny wind would make it dip and wobble, but it recovered again as straight and thin as ever.

"Anything but a good likeness," said Lydia, without, however, lifting her eyes from her book.

"It may come yet," rejoined Ardalion. "Here, I'm going to prune this nostril and we'll get it. Kind of dull light this afternoon."

"What's dull?" inquired Lydia, lifting her eyes and holding one finger on the interrupted line.

Let me interrupt this passage, too, for there is still another piece of my life that summer worthy of your attention, reader. While apologizing for the muddle and mottle of my tale, let me repeat that it is not I who am writing, but my memory, which has its own whims and rules. So, watch me roaming again about the forest near Ardalion's lake; this time I have come alone and not by car, but by train (as far as Koenigsdorf) and bus (as far as the yellow post).

On the suburban map Ardalion left on our balcony one day all the features of the locality stand out very clear. Let us suppose I am holding that map before me; then the city of Berlin, which is outside the picture, may be imagined somewhere in the vicinity of my left elbow. On the map itself, in its southwestern corner, there stretches northward, like a black and white bit of scaled tape, the railway line, which, metaphysically at least, runs along my sleeve cuffward from Berlin. My wristwatch is the small town of Koenigsdorf, beyond which the black and white ribbon turns and proceeds eastward, where there is another circle (the lower button of my waistcoat): Eichenberg.

No need, however, to travel as far as that yet; we get off at Koenigsdorf. As the railway line swerves to the east, its companion, the main road, leaves it and continues north alone, straight to the village of Waldau (the nail of my left thumb). Thrice a day there is a bus plying between Koenigsdorf and Waldau (seventeen kilometers); and it is at Waldau, by the bye, that the center of the land-selling enterprise is situated; a gaily painted pavilion, a fancy flag flapping, numerous yellow signposts: one, for instance, points "to the bathing beach," but there is yet no beach to speak of—only a bog on the lip of the Waldau lake; another points "to the casino," but the latter is likewise absent, though represented by something looking like a tabernacle, with an incipient coffee stall; still another sign invites you "to the sports ground," and sure enough you find there, newly erected, a complicated affair for gymnastics, rather like gallows, but there is nobody who might use the thing, apart from some village urchin swinging head downward and showing the patch on his bottom; and all around, in every direction, lie the lots; some of them are half sold and on Sundays you see fat men in bathing suits and horn-rimmed glasses sternly engaged in building rudimentary bungalows; here and there you may even see flowers freshly planted, or else a pink privy enlaced with climbing roses.

We shall, however, not go as far as Waldau either, but leave the bus on the tenth kilometer from Koenigsdorf, at a point where a solitary yellow post stands on our right. On the east side of the highway the map shows a vast space all dotted over: it is the forest; there, in its very heart, lies the small lake we bathed in, with, on its western bank, spread fanwise like playing cards, a dozen allotments, only one of which is sold (Ardalion's—if you can call it sold).

We are now getting to the exciting part. Mention has already been made of the station of Eichenberg which comes after Koenigsdorf when you travel east. Now comes a technical question: can a person starting from the neighborhood of Ardalion's lake reach Eichenberg on foot? The answer is: yes. We should go round the southern side of the lake and then bear east through the wood. After a four-kilometer walk, keeping in the wood all the time, we come out to a rustic lane, one end of which leads no matter where, to hamlets we need not bother about, while the other brings us to Eichenberg.

My life is all mangled and messed, but here I am clowning away, juggling with bright little descriptions, playing on the cosy pronoun "we," winking at the tourist, the cottage owner, the lover of Nature, that picturesque hash of greens and blues. But be patient with me, my reader. The walk we shall presently take will be your rich reward. These conversations with readers are quite silly too. Stage asides. The eloquent hiss: "Soft now! Someone is coming. . . ."

That walk. I was dropped by the bus at the yellow post. The bus resumed its course taking away from me three old women in polka-dotted black; a fellow wearing a velvet waistcoat, with a scythe wrapped in sackcloth; a small girl with a large parcel; and a man in an overcoat despite the heat, with a heavy-looking traveling bag on his knees: probably a veterinary surgeon.

Among the spurge and scutch-grass I found traces of tires —the tires of my car which had bumped and bounced here several times, during the trips we had made. I wore plus fours, or as Germans call them: "knickerbockers" (the "k" is sounded). I entered the wood. I stopped at the exact spot where I and my wife had once waited for Ardalion. I smoked a cigarette there. I looked at the little puff of smoke that slowly stretched out in midair, was folded by ghostly fingers, and melted away. I felt a spasm in my throat. I went on to the lake and noticed, on the sand, a crumpled black and orange scrap of film wrap (Lydia had been snapping us). I went round the lake on its south side and then straight east through the thick pine wood.

After an hour's stroll I came out on the country road. I took it and in another hour was in Eichenberg. I boarded a slow train. I returned to Berlin.

Several times I repeated this monotonous walk without ever meeting a soul in the forest. Gloom and a deep hush. The land near the lake was not selling at all; indeed, the whole enterprise was in a bad way. When we three used to go out there for a swim, our solitude all day long remained so perfect that one could, if a body desired, bathe stark naked; which reminds me that once, at my order, frightened Lydia peeled off her bathing suit and, with many a pretty blush and nervous giggle, posed in the buff and the brown (fat thighs so tightly pressed together she could hardly stand) for her portrait before Ardalion, who all of a sudden got huffed about something, probably about his own lack of talent and, abruptly ceasing to draw, stalked away to look for edible toadstools.

As to my portrait, he worked at it stubbornly, continuing well into August, when, having failed to cope with the honest slog of charcoal, he changed to the petty knavishness of pastel. I set myself a certain time limit: the date of his finishing the thing. At last there came the pear-juice aroma of lacquer, the portrait was framed, and Lydia gave Ardalion twenty German marks, slipping them, for the sake of elegancy, into an envelope. We had guests that evening, Orlovius

among others, and we all stood and gaped; at what? At the
ruddy horror of my face. I do not know why he had lent my
cheeks that fruity hue; they are really as pale as death. Look
as one might, none could see the ghost of a likeness! How
utterly ridiculous, for instance, that crimson point in the
canthus, or that glimpse of eyetooth from under a curled,
snarly lip. All this—against an ambitious background hinting
at things that might have been either geometrical figures or
gallow trees. . . .

Orlovius, with whom shortsightedness was a form of stupidity, went up to the portrait as close as he could and after
having pushed his spectacles up on his forehead (why ever did
he wear them? They were only a hindrance) stood quite still
with half-opened mouth, gently panting at the picture as if
he were about to make a meal of it. "The modern style," he
said at length with disgust and passed to its neighbor, which
he began to examine with the same conscientious attention,
although it was but an ordinary print found in every Berlin
home: "The Isle of the Dead."

And now, dear reader, let us imagine a smallish office room
on the sixth story of an impersonal house. The typist had
gone; I was alone. In the window a cloudy sky loomed. On
the wall a calendar showed a huge black nine, rather like the
tongue of a bull: the ninth of September. Upon the table
lay the worries of the day (in the guise of letters from creditors) and among them stood a symbolically empty chocolate
box with the lilac lady who had been untrue to me. Nobody
about. I uncovered the typewriter. All was quiet. On a certain
page of my pocket diary (destroyed since) there was a certain
address, written in a half-illiterate hand. Looking through
that trembling prism I could see a waxen brow bending, a

dirty ear; head downwards, a violet dangled from a button-hole; a black-nailed finger pressed upon my silver pencil.

I remember, I shook off that numbness, put the little book back into my pocket, took out my keys, was about to lock up and leave—*was* leaving, but then stopped in the passage with my heart going pit-a-pit.... No, it was impossible to leave. ... I returned to the room and stood awhile by the window looking at the house opposite. Lamps had already lit up there, shining upon office ledgers, and a man in black, with one hand behind his back, was walking to and fro, presumably dictating to a secretary I could not see. Ever and anon he appeared, and once, even, he stopped at the window to do some thinking, and then again turned, dictating, dictating, dictating.

Inexorable! I switched on the light, sat down, pressed my temples. Suddenly, with mad fury, the telephone rang; but it proved a mistake—wrong number. And then there was silence once more, save for the light patter of the rain quickening the approach of night.

# Chapter Four

"Dear Felix, I have found some work for you. First of all we must have an eye-to-eye monologue and get things settled. As I happen to be going to Saxony on business, I suggest that you meet me at Tarnitz, which I hope is not far from your present whereabouts. Let me know without delay whether my plan suits you. If it does, I shall tell you the day, the hour and the exact place, and send you such money as your coming may cost you. The traveling life I lead prevents me from having any fixed abode, so you had better direct your answer 'post office' (here follows the address of a Berlin post office) with the word 'Ardalion' on the envelope. Good-bye for the present. I expect to hear from you." (No signature.)

Here it is before me, the letter I finally wrote on that ninth of September, 1930. I cannot recollect now if the "monologue" was a slip or a joke. The thing is typed out on good, eggshell blue notepaper with a frigate for watermark; but it is now sadly creased and soiled at the corners; vague imprints of his fingers, perhaps. Thus it would seem that I were the receiver—not the sender. Well, so it ought to be in the long run, for haven't we changed places, he and I?

There are in my possesssion two more letters written on similar paper, but all the *answers* have been destroyed. If I still had them—if I had, for instance, that idiotic one which, with beautifully timed nonchalance, I showed to Orlovius (and then destroyed like the rest), it would be possible now to adopt an epistolic form of narration. A time-honored form with great achievements in the past. From Ex to Why: "Dear Why"—and above you are sure to find the date. The letters come and go—quite like the ding-dong flight of a ball over a net. The reader soon ceases to pay any attention whatever to the dates; and indeed what does it matter to him whether a given letter was written on the ninth of September or on September the sixteenth? Dates are required, however, to keep up the illusion.

So it goes on and on, Ex writing to Why and Why to Ex, page after page. Sometimes an outsider, a Zed, intrudes and adds his own little contribution to the correspondence, but he does so with the sole aim of making clear to the reader (not looking at him the while except for an occasional squint) some event, which, for reasons of plausibility and the like, neither Ex nor Why could very well have explained.

They, too, write with circumspection: all those "do-you-remember-that-time-whens" (detailed recollections follow) are brought in, not so much with the object of refreshing Why's memory as in order to give the reader the required reference —so that, on the whole, the effect produced is rather droll, those neatly inscribed and perfectly unnecessary dates, being, as I have already said, especially good fun. And when at last Zed butts in suddenly with a letter to his own personal correspondent (for it is a world consisting of correspondents that such novels imply) telling him of Ex's and Why's death or else of their fortunate union, the reader finds himself feeling that he would prefer the most ordinary missive from the tax collector to all this. As a rule I have always been noted for my exceptional humorousness; it goes naturally with a fine imagination; woe to the fancy which is not accompanied by wit.

One moment. I was copying that letter and now it has vanished somewhere.

I can continue; it had slipped under the table.

A week later the answer arrived (I had been to the post office five times and my nerves were on edge): Felix informed me that he gratefully accepted my suggestion. As often happens with uneducated people, the tone of his letter was in complete disagreement with that of his usual conversation: his epistolary voice was a tremulous falsetto with lapses of eloquent huskiness whereas in real life he had a self-satisfied baritone sinking to a didactic bass.

I wrote to him again, this time enclosing a ten-mark note, and asking him to meet me on the first of October at five P.M. near the bronze equestrian statue at the end of the boulevard which starts left of the railway-station square, at Tarnitz. I did not remember either that bronze rider's identity (some vulgar and mediocre *Herzog*, I believe), or the name of the boulevard, but one day, while driving through Saxony in the car of a business acquaintance, I got stranded for two hours at Tarnitz, my companion trying to perform some complicated telephoning; and as I have always possessed a memory of the camera type, I caught and fixed that street, that statue and other details—quite a small-size photo, really; though if I knew of a way of enlarging it, one might even discern the lettering of the shop signs, for that apparatus of mine is of admirable quality.

My letter of "Sept. the 16th" is handwritten: I dashed it off at the post office, being so excited by receiving a reply to "mine of the 9th inst.," that I had not the patience to wait till I got to a typewriter. Also, there was yet no special reason to be shy of any of my several hands, for I knew that I should prove the recipient eventually. After posting the letter, I felt what probably a purple red-veined thick maple leaf feels, during its slow flutter from branch to brook.

A few days before the first of October I happened to walk with my wife through the Tiergarten; there on a foot bridge we stopped, with our elbows upon the railing. Below, on the still surface of the water, we admired the exact replica (ignoring the model, of course) of the park's autumn tapestry of many-hued foliage, the glassy blue of the sky, the dark outlines of the parapet and of our inclined faces. When a slow leaf fell, there would flutter up to meet it, out of the water's shadowy depths, its unavoidable double. Their meeting was soundless. The leaf came twirling down, and twirling up there would rise towards it, eagerly, its exact, beautiful, lethal reflection. I could not tear my gaze away from those inevitable meetings. "Come on," said Lydia and sighed. "Autumn, autumn," she said after a while, "Autumn. Yes, it is autumn." She already wore her leopard-spotted fur coat. I lagged behind and pierced fallen leaves with my cane.

"How lovely it ought to be in Russia now," she said (similar utterances came from her in early spring and on fine winter days: summer weather alone had no action at all upon her imagination).

". . . There is no bliss on earth. . . . There's peace and freedom, though. . . . An enviable lot long have I yearned to know. Long have I, weary slave—"

"Come on, weary slave. We are dining a little earlier."

". . . been contemplating flight. . . . You'd probably find it dull, Lydia—without Berlin, without Ardalion's vulgar rot?"

"Why, no. I want awfully to go somewhere too. . . . Sunshine, sea waves. A nice cosy life. Can't understand why you should criticize him so."

"... 'Tis time, my dear, 'tis time.... The heart demands repose.... Oh, no, I'm not criticizing him. By the way, what could we do with that monstrous portrait? It is an absolute eyesore. Day after day flits by ..."

"Look, Hermann, people on horseback. I'm sure she thinks she's a beauty, that female. Oh, come on, walk. You are dragging along like a sulky child. Really, you know, I am very fond of him. I have long wanted to give him a lot of money for a trip to Italy."

"... An enviable lot ... Long have I ... Nowadays Italy would not help a bad painter. It may have been like that once, long ago. Long have I, weary slave ..."

"You seem quite asleep, Hermann. Do let us buck up, please."

Now, I want to be quite frank: I did not experience any special craving for a rest; but latterly such had become the standing topic between me and my wife. Barely did we find ourselves alone than with blunt obstinacy I turned the conversation towards "the abode of pure delight"—as that Pushkin poem has it.

Meanwhile I counted the days with impatience. I had put off the appointment till the first of October, because I wanted to give myself a chance of changing my mind; and I cannot help thinking today that if I *had* changed my mind and not gone to Tarnitz, Felix would still be loitering about the bronze duke, or resting on a neighboring bench, drawing with his stick, from left to right and from right to left, the earthen rainbows drawn by every man with a stick and time to spare (our eternal subjection to the circle in which we are all imprisoned!). Yes, thus he would still be sitting to this day, and I would keep remembering him, with wild anguish and passion; a huge aching tooth and nothing with which to pull it out; a woman whom one cannot possess; a place, which, owing to the peculiar topography of nightmares, keeps agonizingly out of reach.

On the eve of my departure, Ardalion and Lydia were playing patience, whereas I paced the rooms and surveyed myself in all the mirrors. At that time I was still on admirable terms with mirrors. During the last fortnight I had let my mustache grow. This altered my countenance for the worse. Above my bloodless mouth there bristled a brownish-red blotch with an obscene little notch in the middle. I had the sensation that it was glued on; and sometimes it seemed to me that a small prickly animal was settled on my upper lip. At night, half asleep, I would suddenly pluck at my face, and my fingers did not recognize it. So, as I was saying, I paced about and smoked, and out of every speckly psyche in the flat there glanced at me, with eyes both apprehensive and grave, a hastily made-up individual. Ardalion, in a blue shirt with a pseudo-Scotch tie, clapped down card after card, like a tavern gambler. Lydia sat sideways to the table, legs crossed, skirt up to above stocking line, and exhaled the smoke of her cigarette upward, with her underlip thrust out and her eyes fixing the cards on the table. It was a black and boisterous night; every five seconds there would come, skimming across the roofs, the pale beam of the Radio Tower: a luminous twitch; the mild lunacy of a revolving search-light. Through the narrow window ajar in the bathroom there arrived from some window across the yard, the creamy voice of a broadcaster. In the dining room the lamp illumined my hideous portrait. Blue-shirted Ardalion clapped down the cards; Lydia sat with her elbow on the table; smoke rose from the ashtray. I stepped out on to the balcony.

"Shut the door—there's a draught," came Lydia's voice from the dining room. A sharp wind made the stars blink and flicker. I returned indoors.

"Whither is our pretty one going?" asked Ardalion without addressing either of us.

"To Dresden," replied Lydia.

They were now playing *durachki*, dupes.

"My kindest regards to the Sistine," said Ardalion. "No, I can't cover that, I'm afraid. Let's see. This way."

"He'd do better if he went to bed, he's dead-tired," said Lydia. "Look here, you've no right to feel the pack, it's dishonest."

"I didn't mean to," said Ardalion. "Don't be cross, pussy. And is he going for long?"

"This one too, Ardy dear, this one too, please, you haven't covered it, either."

So they went on for a good while, talking now of their cards and now about me, as though I were not in the room or as though I were a shadow, a ghost, a dumb creature; and that joking habit of theirs, which before used to leave me indifferent, now seemed to me loaded with meaning, as if indeed it were merely my reflection that was present, my real body being far away.

Next day in the afternoon, I got out at Tarnitz. I had a suitcase with me, and it hampered my movements, for I belong to that class of men who hate carrying anything; what I like is to display expensive fawn gloves, spreading my fingers and swinging my arms freely, as I saunter along and turn out the glistening toes of my handsomely shod feet, which are small for my size and very smart in their mouse-

[ 65 ]

grey spats, for spats are similar to gloves in that they lend a man mellow elegance akin to the special cachet of high-class traveling articles.

I love those shops where suitcases are sold, smelling good, creaking; the virginity of pig leather under the protective cloth; but I am digressing, digressing—maybe I *want* to digress ... never mind, let us go on, where was I? Yes, I resolved to leave my bag at the hotel. What hotel? I crossed the square, looking about me not only for a hotel, but also attempting to recall the place, as I had passed there once and remembered that boulevard yonder and the post office. I had no time, however, to exercise my memory. All of a sudden my vision was crowded with the signboard of a hotel, its entrance, a pair of laurel bushes in green tubs on either side ... but that hint at luxury proved to be a deception, for as soon as you went in, you were knocked silly by the reek from the kitchen; two hirsute nincompoops were drinking beer at the bar, and an old waiter, squatting on his haunches and wagging the end of the napkin under his armpit, was rolling on the floor a fat, white-bellied pup, which was wagging its tail too.

I asked for a room (adding that my brother might spend the night with me) and was given a fair-sized one with a couple of beds and a decanter of dead water on a round table, as at the chemist's. The waiter gone, I stood there more or less alone, my ears ringing and a feeling of strange surprise pervading me. My double was probably already in the same town as I; was already waiting, maybe, in that town; consequently, I was represented by two persons. Were it not for my mustache and clothes, the hotel staff might—but maybe (I went on, skipping from thought to thought) his features had altered and now were no longer like mine, and

I had come in vain. "Please, God!" I said with force, and failed to understand, myself, why I said so; for did not the sense of my whole life consist now in my possessing a live reflection? So why then did I mention the name of a non-existent God, why did there flash through my mind the foolish hope that my reflection had been distorted?

I went to the window and looked out: there was a dreary courtyard down there and a round-backed Tartar in an embroidered skullcap was showing a small blue carpet to a buxom barefooted woman. Now I knew that woman and I recognized that Tartar too, and the patch of weeds in one corner of the yard, and that vortex of dust, and the Caspian wind's soft pressure, and the pale sky sick of looking on fisheries.

At that moment there was a knock, a maid entered with the additional pillow and the cleaner chamber pot I had demanded, and when I turned to the window again it was no longer a Tartar whom I saw there but some local peddler selling braces, and the woman was gone. But while I looked there started afresh that process of fusion, of building, that making up of a definite remembrance; there reappeared, growing and clustering, those weeds in a corner of the yard, and again red-haired Christina Forsmann, whom I had known carnally in 1915, fingered the Tartar's carpet, and sand flew, and I could not discover what the kernel was, around which all those things were formed, and where exactly the germ, the fount—suddenly I glanced at the decanter of dead water and it said "warm"—as in that game when you hide objects; and very possibly I should have finally found the trifle, which, unconsciously noticed by me, had at once set going the engine of memory (or, again, I should not have found it, the simple, nonliterary explanation being that everything in that provincial German hotel chamber, even the view, vaguely and uglily resembled something seen in Russia ages ago) had I not thought of my appointment; and that made me draw on my gloves and hurry out.

I turned down the boulevard, past the post office. A brutal wind was blowing and chasing leaves—scurry, cripples!—athwart the street. In spite of my impatience I was as observant as usual, noting the faces and trousers of passersby, the tramcars which seemed like toys compared to the Berlin ones, the shops, a giant's top hat painted on a peeling wall, signboards, the name of a fishmonger: Carl Spiess, reminding me of one Carl Spiess whom I used to know in that Volga village of my past and who likewise sold spitchcocks.

At last, reaching the end of the street, I saw the bronze horse rearing and using its tail for a prop, like a woodpecker, and if the duke riding it had stretched out his arm with more energy, the whole monument in the murky evening light might have passed for that of Peter the Great in the town he founded. On one of the benches an old man was eating grapes out of a paper bag; on another bench sat two elderly dames; an invalid old woman of enormous size reclined in a Bath chair and listened to their talk, her round eyes agog. Twice and thrice did I go round the statue, observing as I went the snake writhing under that hind hoof, that legend in Latin, that jackboot with the black star of a spur. Sorry, there was really no snake; it was just my fancy borrowing from Tsar Peter—whose statue, anyway, wears buskins.

Then I sat down on an empty bench (there were half a dozen in all) and looked at my watch. Three minutes past five. Sparrows hopped about the turf. On a ridiculously curved flowerbed there grew the filthiest flowers in the world; Michaelmas daisies. Ten minutes elapsed. No, my agitation refused to keep seated. Moreover, I was out of cigarettes and craved frantically for a smoke.

I turned into a side street, passing, as I did so, a black Protestant church which affected an air of antiquity, and espied a tobacconist's. The automatic bell continued to whirr after my entering, as I had not closed the door: "Will you please—" said the bespectacled woman behind the counter, and I stepped back and shut the door sharply. Just above it was one of Ardalion's still-life pictures: a tobacco pipe, on green cloth, and two roses.

"How on earth did you—?" I asked with a laugh. She did not understand at first, and then answered:

"My niece painted it—my niece who died recently."

Well, I'm damned! (thought I). For had I not seen something very similar, if not identical, among Ardalion's pictures? Well, I'm damned!

"Oh, I see," said I aloud: "have you got—" I named the brand I usually smoke, paid for the cigarettes and went out.

Twenty minutes past five.

Not daring to return to the assigned place (so giving fate a chance of altering its programme) and still feeling nothing, neither annoyance, nor relief, I walked for a pretty long time down the side street which led me away from the statue, and at every other step I stopped, trying to light my cigarette, but the wind kept filching my light until I took shelter under a porch, thus blasting the blast—what a pun! I stood under the porch and looked at two little girls playing marbles; rolling by turn the iridescent orb, now bending to give it a push with the back of the finger, now compressing it between the feet to release it with a hop, and all this in order that the marble should trickle into a tiny pit in the ground under a double-trunked birch tree; as I stood looking at that con-

centrated, silent and minute game, I somehow found myself
thinking that Felix could not come for the simple reason
that he was a product of my imagination, which hankered
after reflections, repetitions, masks, and that my presence in
a remote little town was absurd and even monstrous.

Well do I remember that little town—and feel oddly per-
plexed: should I go on giving instances of such aspects of it,
which in a horribly unpleasant way echoed things I had
somewhere seen long ago? It even seems to me now that it
was, that town, constructed of certain refuse particles of my
past, for I discovered in it things most remarkably and most
uncannily familiar to me: a low pale-blue house, the exact
counterpart of which I had seen in a St. Petersburg surburb;
an old-clothes shop, where suits hung that had belonged to
dead acquaintances of mine; a street lamp bearing the same
number (I always like to notice the numbers of street lamps)
as one that had stood in front of the Moscow house where
I lodged; and nearby the same bare birch tree with the same
forked trunk in an iron corset (ah, that is what made me
look at the number on the lamp). I could, if I chose, give
many more examples of that kind, some of which are so subtle,
so—how shall I put it? . . . abstractly personal, as to be unintelligible to the reader, whom I pet and pamper like a
devoted nurse. Nor am I quite certain of the exceptionality
of the aforesaid phenomena. Every man with a keen eye is
familiar with those anonymously retold passages from his
past life: false-innocent combinations of details, which smack
revoltingly of plagiarism. Let us leave them to the conscience
of fate and return, with a sinking heart and dull reluctance,
to the monument at the end of the street.

The old man had finished his grapes and was gone; the
woman, dying from dropsy, had been wheeled away; there

was nobody about, save one man, who sat on that very same bench where I had been sitting a while ago. Leaning forward a little and with knees set apart, he was dealing out crumbs to the sparrows. His stick, which was carelessly set against the seat near his left hip, came slowly into motion the moment I noticed its presence; it started sliding and plopped down on the gravel. The sparrows flew up, described a curve and settled on the surrounding shrubs. I became aware that the man had turned towards me.

You are right, my intelligent reader.

# Chapter Five

Keeping my eyes fixed on the ground, I shook his right hand with my left, simultaneously picked up the fallen stick, and sat down on the bench beside him.

"You are late," I said, without looking at him. He laughed. Still without looking, I unbuttoned my overcoat, removed my hat, passed my palm across my head. I felt hot all over. The wind had died in the madhouse.

"I recognized you at once," said Felix in a fawning idiotically conspirant manner.

I was looking now at the stick in my hands. It was a stout, weathered stick, with its lime wood notched in one place and the owner's name neatly branded on it: "Felix so and so," and under that the date, and then the name of his village. I put it back on the bench, with the fleeting thought that he had come on foot, the rascal.

At last, bracing myself, I turned toward him. Still, it was not at once that I glanced at his face; I started working from his feet upward, as one sees on the screen when the cameraman is trying to be tantalizing. First came big, dusty shoes, thick socks sloppy about the ankles, then shiny blue trousers (the corduroy ones having presumably rotted) and a hand holding a crust of dry bread. Then a blue coat over a dark-grey sweater. Still higher the soft collar that I knew (though now comparatively clean). There I stopped. Should I leave him headless or go on building him? Taking cover behind my hand I glanced between my fingers at his face.

For a moment I had the impression that it had all been a delusion, a hallucination—that never could he have been my double, that gump, with his raised eyebrows, expectantly leering, not quite knowing yet what countenance to assume—therefore raising those eyebrows, so as to be on the safe side. For a moment, as I say, he appeared to me as like me as any man. But then, their fright over, the sparrows returned, one of them hopping quite close, and that diverted his attention; his features fell back to their proper position, and I saw, once again, the marvel that had arrested me five months before.

He flung a handful of crumbs to the sparrows. The nearest made a flurried peck, the crumb sprang up and was nabbed by another, which immediately flew away. Felix again turned to me with his former expectant and cringing servility.

"That one got nothing," said I, pointing to a little chap standing apart and clicking his beak helplessly.

"He's young," observed Felix. "Look, he has hardly any tail yet. I like birdies," he added with a mawkish grin.

"Been in the war?" I queried; and several times running, I cleared my throat, for my voice was hoarse.

"Yes," he answered. "Two years. Why?"

"Oh, nothing. Damned afraid of getting killed, eh?"

He winked and spoke with evasive obscurity:

"Every mouse has a house, but it's not every mouse that comes out."

In German the end rhymed too; I had already noticed his fondness for insipid sayings; and it was quite useless racking one's brains trying to see the idea he really desired to express.

"That's all. There is no more for you," said he in an aside

to the sparrows. "I like squirrels too" (again that wink). "It's good when a wood is full of squirrels. I like 'em because they are against the landowners. And moles."

"What about sparrows?" I asked with great gentleness. "Are they 'against' as you put it?"

"A sparrow is a beggar among birds—a real street-beggar. A beggar," he repeated again and again, now leaning with both hands on his stick and swaying a little. It was obvious he considered himself to be an extraordinarily astute arguer. No, he was not merely a fool, he was a fool of the melancholic type. Even his smile was glum—made one sick to look at it. And nevertheless I looked greedily. It interested me hugely to observe how our remarkable likeness got broken by the working of his face. If he were to attain old age, I reflected, his grins and grimaces would end by eroding completely our resemblance which is now so perfect when his face freezes.

Hermann (playfully): "Ah, you are a philosopher, I see."

That seemed to offend him a little. "Philosophy is the invention of the rich," he objected with deep conviction. "And all the rest of it has been invented too: religion, poetry . . . oh, maiden, how I suffer, oh, my poor heart! I don't believe in love. Now, friendship—that's another matter. Friendship and music.

"I'll tell you something," he went on, laying his stick aside and addressing me with some heat. "I'd like to have a friend who'd always be ready to share his slice of bread with me and who'd bequeath to me a piece of land, a cottage. Yes, I'd like to have a real friend. I'd work for him as a gardener, and then afterwards his garden would become mine, and I'd always remember my dead comrade with grateful tears. We'd fiddle together, or, say, he'd play the flute and I the mandolin.

[ 75 ]

But women . . . now, really, could you name a single one who did not deceive her husband?"

"All very true! Very true indeed. It's a pleasure to hear you talk. Did you ever go to school?"

"Just for a short time. What can one learn at school? Nothing. If a fellow is clever, what good are lessons to him? The chief thing is Nature. Politics, for instance, don't attract me. And generally speaking . . . the world, you know, is *dirt.*"

"A perfectly logical conclusion," said I. "Yes—your logic is faultless. Quite surprisingly so. Now, look here, clever, just hand me back that pencil of mine and be quick about it."

That made him sit up and put him into the frame of mind I required.

"You forgot it on the grass," he mumbled in a bewildered manner. "I didn't know if I'd see you again."

"Stole it and sold it!" I cried—even stamped my foot.

His reply was remarkable: first he shook his head denying the theft and then immediately nodded admitting the transaction. There was gathered in him, I believe, the whole bouquet of human stupidity.

"Confound you," I said, "be more circumspect next time. Well, anyway, let's let bygones— Have a cigarette."

He relaxed and beamed, as he saw my wrath had passed; started to display gratitude: "Thank you, oh, thank you. Now, really, how marvelously alike we are! Mightn't one suppose my father had sinned with your mother?" And he laughed wheedlingly, very pleased with his joke.

"To business," said I, affecting a sudden bluff gravity. "I have invited you here not merely for the ethereal delights of small talk. I spoke in my letter of the help I was going to give you, of the work I had found for you. First of all, however, let me put you one question. Your answer must be candid and exact. Tell me, what do you think I am?"

Felix examined me, then turned away and shrugged his shoulders.

"It's not a riddle I'm setting you," I went on patiently. "I perfectly realize that you cannot know my identity. Let us, in any case, waive aside the possibility you so wittily mentioned. Our blood, Felix, is not the same. No, my good chap, not the same. I was born a thousand miles from your cradle and the honor of my parents—as of yours, I hope—is unstained. You are an only son: So am I. Consequently neither to me nor to you can there come that mysterious creature: a long-lost brother once stolen by the gypsies. No ties unite us; I have no obligations toward you, mark that well, no obligations whatever; if I intend helping you, I do so of my own free will. Bear that in mind, please. Now, let me ask you again: what do you suppose I am? What is the opinion you have formed of me? For you must have formed *some* kind of opinion, mustn't you?"

"Maybe you're an actor," said Felix dubiously.

"If I understand you aright, friend, you mean that at our first meeting you thought: 'Ah, he is probably one of those theatrical blokes, the dashing kind, with funny fancies and fine clothes; maybe a celebrity.' Am I correct?"

Felix fixed the toe of his shoe with which he was smoothing the gravel, and his face assumed a rather strained expression.

"I didn't think anything," he said peevishly. "I simply saw —well, that you were sort of curious about me, and so on. And do you actors get well paid?"

A tiny note: the idea he gave me appeared to me subtle; the singular bend which it took brought it into contact with the main part of my plan.

"You've guessed," I exclaimed, "you've guessed. Yes, I'm an actor. A film actor, to be accurate. Yes, that's right. You put it nicely, splendidly! What else can you say about me?"

Here I noticed that somehow his spirits had fallen. My profession seemed to have disappointed him. There he sat frowning moodily with the half-smoked cigarette held between finger and thumb. Suddenly he lifted his head, blinked.

"And what kind of work do you want to offer me?" he inquired without his former ingratiating sweetness.

"Not so fast, not so fast. All in its proper time. I was asking you what else did you think of me? Come, answer me. Please."

"Oh, well ... I know you like traveling; that's about all."

In the meantime night was approaching; the sparrows had long disappeared; the monument loomed darker and seemed to have grown in size. From behind a black tree there came out noiselessly a gloomy and fleshful moon. A cloud slipped a mask over it in passing, which left visible only its chubby chin.

"Well, Felix, it's getting dark and dismal out here. I bet you are hungry. Come on, let us find something to eat and go on with our talk over a pint of ale. Does that suit you?"

"It does," said Felix in a slightly livelier voice and then added sententiously: "A hungry belly has no ears" (I translate his adages anyhow; in German they all jingled with rhymes).

We got up and advanced towards the yellow lights of the boulevard. As night fell, I was hardly aware of our resemblance. Felix slouched beside me, seemingly deep in thought and his mode of walking was as dull as himself.

I queried: "Have you ever been to Tarnitz before?"

"No," he answered. "I don't care for towns. Me and my likes find towns tiresome."

The sign of a pothouse. Standing in the window a barrel, guarded by two bearded brownies of terra-cotta. As good as any other. We entered and chose a table in a far corner. As I withdrew the glove from my hand, I surveyed the place with a searching eye. There were only three people and these paid no attention to us whatever. The waiter came up, a pale little man with pince-nez (it was not the first time I had seen a pince-nez'd waiter, but I could not recall where and when I had seen one before). While awaiting our order, he looked at me, then at Felix. Naturally, owing to my mustache, our likeness did not leap to the eyes; and indeed, I had let my mustache grow with the special purpose of not attracting undue attention when appearing together with Felix. There is, I believe, somewhere in Pascal a wise thought: that two persons resembling each other do not present any interest when met singly, but create quite a stir when both appear at once. I have never read Pascal nor do I remember where I pinched that quotation. Oh, I used to thrive on such monkey-tricks in my youth! Unfortunately I was not alone in making a show of this or that pickpocket maxim. In St. Petersburg once, at a party, I remarked: "There are feelings, says Turgenev, which may be expressed only by music." A few minutes later there arrived one more guest, who, in the middle of the conversation, delivered the very same phrase, lifted from the program of a concert at which I had noticed him heading for the greenroom. He, and not I, made an ass of himself, to be sure; still, it produced an uncomfortable feeling in me (though I derived some relief from asking him slyly how he had liked the great Viabranova), so I decided to cut out the highbrow business. All this is a digression and not an evasion—most emphatically not an evasion; for I fear nothing and will tell all. It should be admitted that I exercise an exquisite control not only over myself but over my style of writing. How many novels I wrote when young—just like that, casually, and without the least intention of publishing them. Here is another utterance: a published manuscript, says Swift, is comparable to a whore. I happened one day (in Russia) to give Lydia a manuscript of mine to read, telling her that it was the work of a friend; she found it boring and did not finish it. To this day my handwriting is practically unfamiliar to her. I have exactly twenty-five kinds of handwritings, the best (i.e., those I use the most readily) being as follows: a round diminutive one with a pleasant plumpness about its curves, so that every word looks like a newly baked fancy-cake; then a fast cursive, sharp and nasty, the scribble of a hunchback in a hurry, with no dearth of abbreviations; then a suicide's hand, every letter a noose, every comma a trigger; then the one I prize most: big, legible, firm and absolutely impersonal; thus might write the abstract hand in its superhuman cuff, which one finds figured on signposts and in textbooks of physics. It was in such a hand that I began writing the book now offered to the reader; soon, however, my pen ran amok: this book is written in all my twenty-five hands mixed together, so that the typesetter or some typist, unknown to me, or again the definite person I have elected, that Russian author to whom my manuscript will be forwarded when the time comes, might think that several people participated in the writing of my book; and it is also extremely probable that some rat-faced, sly little expert will discover in its cacographic orgy a sure sign of psychic abnormality. So much the better.

There ... I have mentioned you, my first reader, you, the well-known author of psychological novels. I have read them and found them very artificial, though not badly constructed. What will you feel, reader-writer, when you tackle my tale? Delight? Envy? Or even . . . who knows? . . . you may use my termless removal to give out my stuff for your own . . . for the fruit of your own crafty . . . yes, I grant you that . . . crafty and experienced imagination; leaving me out in the cold. It would not be hard for me to take in advance proper measures against such impudence. Whether I *shall* take them, that is another question. What if I find it rather flattering that you should steal my property? Theft is the best compliment one can possibly pay a thing. And do you know the most amusing part? I assume that, having made up your mind to effect that pleasant robbery, you will suppress the compromising lines, the very lines I am writing now, and, moreover, fashion certain bits to your liking (which is a less pleasant thought) just as a motorcar thief repaints the car he has stolen. And, in this respect, I shall allow myself to relate a little story, which is certainly the funniest little story I know.

Some ten days ago, that is, about the tenth of March 1931 (half a year has suddenly gone—a fall in a dream, a run in time's stocking), a person, or persons, passing along the highway or through the wood (that, I think, will be settled in due course) espied, on its edge, and unlawfully took possession of, a small blue car of such and such a make and power (I leave out the technical details). And, as a matter of fact, that is all.

I do not claim that this story has universal appeal: its point is none too obvious. It made *me* scream with laughter only because I was in the know. I may add that nobody told it me, nor have I read it anywhere; what I did was, really, to deduce it by means of some close reasoning from the bare fact of the car's disappearance, a fact quite wrongly interpreted by the papers. Back again, time!

"Can you drive?" was, I remember, the question I suddenly put to Felix, when the waiter, failing to notice anything particular about us, placed before me a lemonade and before Felix a tankard of beer, into the profuse froth of which my blurred double eagerly dipped his upper lip.

"What?" he uttered, with a beatific grunt.

"I was asking if you can drive a car."

"Can't I just! I once chummed up with a chauffeur who worked at a castle near my village. One fine day we ran over a sow. Lord, how she squealed!"

The waiter brought us some sort of gravy-logged hash, a great deal of it, and mashed potatoes, also drowned in sauce. Where the deuce had I already seen a pince-nez on a waiter's nose? Ah—it comes back to me (only now, while writing this!) —at a rotten little Russian restaurant in Berlin; and that other waiter was very like this one—the same sort of sullen straw-haired little man, but of gentler birth.

"So that's that, Felix. We have eaten and drunk; now, let us talk. You have made certain suppositions concerning me and these have proved correct. Now, before going deeper into the business on hand, I want to sketch out for your benefit a general picture of my personality and life; you won't be long in understanding why it is urgent. To begin with..."

I took a sip and resumed:

"To begin with, I was born of a rich family. We had a house and a garden—ah, what a garden, Felix! Imagine, not merely rose trees but rose thickets, roses of all kinds, each variety bearing a framed label: roses, you know, receive names as resounding as those given to racehorses. Besides roses, there grew in our garden a quantity of other flowers, and when, of a morning, the whole place was brilliant with dew, the sight, Felix, was a dream. When still a child, I loved to look after our garden and well did I know my job: I had a small watering can, Felix, and a small mattock, and my parents would sit in the shade of an old cherry tree, planted by my grandfather, and look on, with tender emotion, at me, the small busybody (just imagine, imagine the picture!) engaged in removing from the roses, and squelching, caterpillars that looked like twigs. We had plenty of farmyard creatures, as, for example, rabbits, the most oval animal of all, if you know what I mean; and choleric turkeys with carbuncular caruncles (I made a gobbling sound) and darling little kids and many, many others.

"Then my parents lost all their money and died, and the lovely garden vanished; and it is only now that happiness seems to have come my way once more: I have lately managed to acquire a bit of land on the edge of a lake, and there will be a new garden still better than the old one. My sappy boyhood was perfumed through and through with all those flowers and fruits, whereas the neighboring wood, huge and thick, cast over my soul a shadow of romantic melancholy.

"I was always lonely, Felix, and I am lonely still. Women . . . No need to talk of those fickle and lewd beings. I have traveled a good deal; just like you, I love to rove with a bag strapped to my shoulders, although, to be sure, there were always certain reasons (which I wholly condemn) for my wanderings to be more agreeable than yours. It is really a striking thing: have you ever pondered over the following matter?—two men, alike poor, live not alike; one say, as you, frankly and hopelessly leading a beggar's existence, while the other, though quite as poor, living in a very different style—a carefree, well-fed fellow, moving among the gay rich. . . .

"Why is it so? Because, Felix, those two belong to different classes; and speaking of classes, let us imagine a man who travels fourth-class without a ticket and another who travels first, without one either: X sits on a hard bench; Mr. Y lolls on a cushioned seat; but both have empty purses—or, to be precise, Mr. Y has got a purse to show, though empty, whereas X has not even that and can show nothing but holes in the lining of his pocket.

"By speaking thus I am trying to make you grasp the difference between us: I am an actor, living generally on air, but I have always elastic hopes for the future; they may be stretched indefinitely, such hopes, without bursting. You are denied even that; and you would have always remained a pauper, had not a miracle occurred; that miracle is my meeting you.

"There is not a thing, Felix, that one could not exploit. Nay, more: there is not a thing that one could not exploit for a very long time, and very successfully. Maybe in the more fiery of your dreams you saw a number of two figures, the limit of your aspirations. Now, however, the dream does not only come true, but at once runs into three figures. None too easy for your fancy to comprehend, is it, for didn't you feel you were nearing a hardly thinkable infinity when you reckoned above ten? And now we are turning the corner of that infinity, and a century beams at you, and over its shoulder—another; and who knows, Felix, maybe a fourth figure is ripening; yes, it makes the head swim, and the heart beat, and the nerves tingle, but it is true nevertheless. See here: you have grown so used to your miserable fate that I doubt whether you catch my meaning; what I say seems dark to you, and strange; what comes next will seem still darker and stranger."

I spoke a long while in that vein. He kept glancing at me with distrust; quite likely, he had gradually acquired the notion that I was making fun of him. Fellows of his kind remain good-natured up to a certain point only. As it dawns upon them that they are about to be put upon, all their goodness comes off, there appears in their eyes a vitreous glint, they work themselves heavily into a state of solid passion.

I spoke obscurely, but my object was not to infuriate him. On the contrary, I wished to curry favor with him; to perplex, but at the same time to attract; in a word, to convey to him vaguely but cogently the image of a man of his nature and inclinations. My fancy, however, ran riot and that rather disgustingly, with the weighty playfulness of an elderly but still smirking lady who has had a drop too much.

Upon my noting the impression I was making, I stopped for a minute, half sorry I had frightened him, but then, all at once, I felt how sweet it was to be able to make one's listener thoroughly uncomfortable. So I smiled and continued thus:

"You must forgive me, Felix, for all this chatter, but, you see, I seldom have occasion to take my soul for an outing. Then, too, I am in a great hurry to demonstrate myself from all sides, for I want to give you an exhaustive description of the man with whom you will have to work, the more so as the work in question will be directly concerned with our resemblance. Tell me, do you know what an understudy is?"

He shook his head, his lower lip drooped; I had long observed that he breathed preferably through his mouth— his nose being stuffed up, or something.

"If you don't, let me explain. Imagine that the manager of a film company—you have been to the cinema, haven't you?"

"Well, yes. . . ."

"Good. So imagine that such a manager or director ...
Excuse me, friend, you seem to be wanting to say something?"

"Well, I haven't been *often*. When I want to spend money
I find something better than pictures."

"Agreed, but there are people who think differently—if
there weren't, then there wouldn't be such a profession as
mine, would there? So, as I was saying, a director has offered
me, for a small remuneration—something like ten thousand
dollars—just a trifle, certainly, just air, but prices have
dropped nowadays—to act in a film where the hero is a musician. This suits me admirably, as in real life I love music
too, and can play several instruments. On summer evenings
I sometimes take my violin to the nearest grove—but to get
back to the point—an understudy, Felix, is a person who can,
in case of emergency, replace a given actor.

"The actor plays his part, with the camera shooting him;
an insignificant little scene remains to be done; the hero, say,
is to drive past in his car; but he can't, he is in bed with a
bad cold. There is no time to be lost, and so his double takes
over and coolly sails past in the car (splendid that you can
manage cars) and when at last the film is shown, not a single
spectator is aware of the substitution. The better the likeness, the dearer its price. There even exist special companies
whose business consists in supplying movie stars with star
ghosts. And the life of the ghost is fine, seeing he gets a fixed
salary but has to work only occasionally, and not much of
work either—just putting on exactly the same clothes as the
hero, and whizzing past in a smart car, in the hero's stead,
that's all! Naturally an understudy ought not to blab about
his job; there would be the hell of a row if some reporter

got wind of the stratagem and the public learned that a bit of its pet actor's part had been faked. You understand now why I was so delightfully excited at finding in you an exact replica of myself. That has always been one of my fondest dreams. Just think how much it means to me—especially at present when the filming has started, and I, a man of delicate health, am cast for the leading part. If anything happens to me they at once call you, you arrive—"

"Nobody calls me and I arrive nowhere," interrupted Felix.

"Why do you speak like that, my dear chap?" said I, with a note of gentle rebuke.

"Because," said Felix, "it is unkind of you to pull a poor man's leg. First I believed you. I thought you'd offer me some honest work. It's been a long dreary tramp coming here. Look at the state of my soles ... and now, instead of work— no, it doesn't suit me."

"I'm afraid there is a slight misunderstanding," I said softly. "What I'm offering you is neither debasing, nor unduly complicated. We'll sign an agreement. You'll get a hundred marks per month from me. Let me repeat: the job is ridiculously easy; child's play—you know the way children dress up to represent soldiers, ghosts, aviators. Just think: you'll be getting a monthly salary of a hundred marks solely for putting on—very rarely, once a year perhaps—exactly the same clothes I am wearing at present. Now, do you know what we ought to do? Let us fix some date to meet and rehearse some little scene, just to see what it looks like ..."

"I don't know a thing about such matters, and don't care to know," objected Felix rather rudely. "But I'll tell you something; my aunt had a son who played the buffoon at fairs, he boozed and was too fond of girls, and my aunt broke her heart over him until the day when, thank God, he dashed his brains out by missing a flying swing and his wife's hands. All those picture houses and circuses—"

Did it actually go on like this? Am I faithfully following the lead of my memory, or has perchance my pen mixed the steps and wantonly danced away? There is something a shade too literary about that talk of ours, smacking of thumb-screw conversations in those stage taverns where Dostoevski is at home; a little more of it and we should hear that sibilant whisper of false humility, that catch in the breath, those repetitions of incantatory adverbs—and then all the rest of it would come, the mystical trimming dear to that famous writer of Russian thrillers.

It even torments me in a way; that is, it does not only torment me, but quite, quite muddles my mind and, I dare say, is fatal to me—the thought that I have somehow been too cocksure about the power of my pen—do you recognize the modulations of that phrase? You do. As for me, I seem to remember that talk of ours admirably, with all its innuendoes, and *vsyu podnogotnuyu*, "the whole subunguality," the secret under the nail (to use the jargon of the torture chamber, where fingernails were prized off, and a favorite term—enhanced by italics—with our national expert in soul ague and the aberrations of human self-respect). Yes, I remember that talk, but am unable to render it exactly, something clogs me, something hot and abhorrent and quite unbearable, which I cannot get rid of because it is as sticky as a sheet of flypaper into which one has walked naked in a pitch-dark room. And, what is more, you cannot find the light.

No, our conversation was not such as is set down here; that is, the *words* maybe were exactly as stated (again that little gasp), but I have not managed or not dared to render the special noises accompanying it; there occurred queer fadings or clottings of sound; and then again that muttering, that susurration, and, suddenly, a wooden voice clearly pronouncing: "Come, Felix, another drink."

The brown floral design on the wall; an inscription explaining testily that the house was not responsible for lost property; the cardboard rounds serving as bases for beer (with a hurriedly penciled sum across one of them); and the distant bar at which a man drank, legs twisted into a black scroll, and smoke encircling him; all these were commentative notes to our discourse, as meaningless, however, as those in the margins of Lydia's trashy books.

Had the trio sitting by the bloodred window curtain, far from us, had they turned and looked at us, those three quiet and morose carousers, they would have seen: the fortunate brother and the luckless brother: one with a small mustache and sleek hair, the other clean-shaven, but needing a haircut (that ghostly little mane down the scruff of his lean neck); facing each other, both sitting alike; elbows on the table and fists at the cheekbones. Thus we were reflected by the misty and, to all appearances, sick mirror, with a freakish slant, a streak of madness, a mirror that surely would have cracked at once had it chanced to reflect one single genuine human countenance.

Thus we sat and I kept up my persuasive drone; I am a bad speaker, and the oration which I seem to render word by word did not flow with the lissom glide it has on paper. Indeed, it is not really possible to set down my incoherent speech, that tumble and jumble of words, the forlornness of subordinated clauses, which have lost their masters and strayed away, and all the superfluous gibber that gives words a support or a creep hole; but my mind worked so rhythmically and pursued its quarry at such a steady pace, that the impression now left me by the trend of my own words is anything but tangled or garbled. My object, however, was still out of reach. The fellow's resistance, proper to one of limited intelligence and timorous humor, had to be broken down somehow. So seduced was I by the neat naturalness of the theme, that I overlooked the probability of its being distasteful to him and even of its frightening him off as naturally as it had appealed to my fancy.

I do not mean, by that, that I have ever had the least connection with the screen or the stage; in point of fact, the only time I performed was a score of years ago, in a little amateur affair at our squire's country seat (which my father managed). I had to speak only a few words: "The prince bade me announce that he would be here presently. Ah! here he comes," instead of which, full of exquisite delight and all aquiver with glee, I spoke thus: "The prince cannot come: he has cut his throat with a razor"; and, as I spoke, the gentleman in the part of the prince was already coming, with a beaming smile on his gorgeously painted face, and there was a moment of general suspense, the whole world was held up—and to this day I remember how deeply I inhaled the divine ozone of monstrous storms and disasters. But although I have never been an actor in the strict sense of the word, I have nevertheless, in real life, always carried about with me a small folding theatre and have appeared in more than one part, and my acting has always been superfine; and if you think that my prompter's name was Gain—capital G *not* C—then you are mightily mistaken. It is all not so simple, my dear sirs.

In the case of my talk with Felix, however, my performance

proved to be merely a loss of time, for I suddenly realized that if I went on with that monologue about filming, he would get up and leave, returning the ten marks I had sent him; (no, on second thought I believe he would not have returned them—no, never!) The weighty German word for "money" (money in German being gold, in French, silver, in Russian, copper) was mouthed by him with extraordinary reverence, which, curiously, could turn into brutal lust. But he would have certainly gone away, with an I-shan't-be-insulted air!

To be perfectly frank, I do not quite see why everything linked with the theatre or cinema seemed so utterly atrocious to him; strange, foreign—yes, but ... atrocious? Let us try to explain it by the German plebeian's backwardness. The German peasant is old-fashioned and prudish; just try, one day, to walk through a village in nothing but swimming trunks. I *have* tried, so I know what happens; the men stand stock-still, the women titter, hiding their faces, quite like parlor maids in old-world comedies.

I fell silent. Felix was silent too, tracing lines on the table with his finger. He had probably expected me to offer him a gardener's job or that of a chauffeur, and was now disappointed and sulky. I called the waiter and paid. Once again we were pacing the streets. It was a sharp bleak night. Among small clouds curled like astrakhan, a shiny flat moon kept sliding in and out.

"Listen, Felix. Our talk is not finished. We cannot leave it like that. I've booked a room in a hotel; come along, you'll spend the night with me."

He accepted this as his due. Slow as his wits were, he understood that I needed him, and that it was unwise to break off our relations without having arrived at something definite. We again walked past the duplicate of the Bronze Rider. Not a soul did we meet on the boulevard. Not a gleam was there in the houses; had I noticed a single lighted window, I should have supposed that somebody had hanged himself there and left the lamp burning—so unwonted and unwarranted would a light have seemed. We reached the hotel in silence. A collarless sleepwalker let us in. Upon entering the room I again had that sensation of something very familiar; but other matters engaged my mind.

"Sit down." He did so with his fists on his knees; his mouth half opened. I removed my coat and thrusting both hands into my trouser pockets and clinking small change in them, started walking to and fro. I wore, by the bye, a lilac tie flecked with black, which blew up every time I turned on my heel. For some while it continued like that; silence, my pacing, the wind of my motion.

All of a sudden Felix, as if shot dead, let his head fall and began unlacing his shoes. I glanced at his unprotected neck, at the wistful expression of his first vertebra, and it made me feel queer to think that I was about to sleep with my double in one room, under one blanket almost, for the twin beds stood side by side, quite close. Then, too, there came, with a pang, the dreadful idea that his flesh might be tainted by the scarlet blotches of a skin disease or by some crude tattooing; I demanded of his body a minimum of resemblance to mine; as to his face, there was no trouble about *that*.

"Yes, go on, take your things off," said I, walking and veering.

He lifted his head, a nondescript shoe in his hand.

"It is a long while since I've slept in a bed," he said with a smile (don't show your gums, fool). "In a real bed."

"Take off everything," I said impatiently. "You are surely dirty, dusty. I'll give you a shirt to sleep in. But first wash."

Grinning and grunting, perhaps a trifle shy of me, he stripped to the skin and proceeded to douche his armpits over the basin of the cupboardlike washstand. I shot glances at him, examining eagerly that stark-naked man. His back was about as muscular as mine, with a pinker coccyx and uglier buttocks. When he turned I could not help wincing at the sight of his big knobbed navel—but then mine is no beauty either. I doubt he had ever in his life washed his animal parts: they looked fairly plausible as these things go but did not invite close inspection. His toenails were much less abominable than I had expected. He was lean and white, much whiter than his face, thus making it seem that it was my face, still retaining its summer tan, that was affixed to his pale trunk. You could even discern the line round his neck where the head adhered. I derived a keen pleasure from that survey; it set my mind at ease; no special marks stigmatized him.

When, having pulled on the clean shirt I issued him from my suitcase, he went to bed, I sat down at his feet and fixed him with a frank sneer. I do not know what he thought, but that unusual cleanness had mollified him, and in a bashful gush of something, which for all its repulsive sentimentality was quite a tender gesture, he stroked my hand and said— I translate literally: "You're a good fellow."

Without unclenching my teeth I went into shivers of laughter; then, I suppose, the expression of my face struck him as odd, for his eyebrows climbed up and he cocked his head. No longer suppressing my mirth I poked a cigarette into his mouth. It fairly made him choke.

"You ass!" I exclaimed. "Haven't you really guessed that

if I made you come here it was for some important, terribly important matter?" and producing a thousand-mark note from my wallet, and still shaking with merriment, I held it up before the fool's face.

"That's for me?" he asked, and dropped the lighted cigarette; it was as if his fingers had involuntarily parted, ready to snatch.

"You'll burn a hole in the sheet," I said (laughing, laughing). "Or in your precious hide! You seem moved, I see. Yes, this money will be yours, you'll even receive it in advance if you agree to the thing I am going to suggest. How was it you didn't realize that I babbled about movies only to test you, and that I am no actor whatsoever, but a shrewd, hard businessman. Briefly, here is the matter: I intend performing a certain operation, and a slight chance exists of their getting at me later. All suspicions, however, will be at once allayed by the definite proof that at the exact time when the aforesaid operation was performed, I happened to be very far from the spot."

"Robbery?" asked Felix, and a look of strange satisfaction flitted across his face.

"I see you aren't as stupid as I thought," I went on, lowering my voice to a mere murmur. "Evidently you have long had an inkling that there was something fishy. And now you are glad that you weren't mistaken, as every man is glad when the correctness of his guess is confirmed. We both have a weakness for silver objects—that's what you thought, didn't you? Or perchance, what really pleased you was that I turned out to be not a leg puller after all, not a dreamer slightly cracked, but a man who meant business?"

"Robbery?" asked Felix again, with new life in his eyes.

"At any rate, an unlawful action. You shall learn the details in due time. First, let me explain what I want you to do. I have a car. Wearing my clothes you'll sit in that car and drive along a certain road. That's all. You'll get a thousand marks—or if you prefer, two hundred and fifty dollars—for that joyride."

"A thousand?" he repeated after me ignoring the lure of valuta. "And when will you give it me?"

"It'll happen perfectly naturally, my friend. On putting on my coat you'll find my wallet in it, and in the wallet, the cash."

"What must I do next?"

"I've told you. Go for a drive. I'll vanish; you'll be seen, taken for me; you'll return and . . . well, I'll be back, too, with my purpose accomplished. Want me to be more exact? Righto. At a certain hour you will drive through a village, where my face is well known; you won't have to speak to anyone, it will all be a matter of a few minutes. But I'll pay for those few minutes handsomely, just because they'll give me the marvelous opportunity of being in two places at once."

"You'll get caught with the goods," said Felix, "and then the police will be after me; it'll all come out at the trial; you'll squeal."

I laughed: "D'you know, friend, I like the way you at once accepted the notion of my being a crook."

He rejoined, saying that he was not fond of jails; that jails sapped one's youth; and that there was nothing like freedom and the singing of birds. He spoke rather thickly and without the least enmity. After a while he became pensive with his elbow upon the pillow. The room was smelly and quiet. Only a couple of paces or one jump separated his bed from mine. I yawned and, without undressing, lay down the Russian way upon (not under) the featherbed. A quaint little thought tickled me: during the night Felix might kill me and rob me. By straining my foot out and aside, and scraping with my shoe against the wall, I managed to reach the switch; slipped; strained still more, and with my heel kicked out the light.

"And what if it's all a lie?" came his dull voice breaking the silence. "What if I don't believe you?"

I did not stir.

"A lie," he repeated a minute later.

I did not stir, and presently I began to breathe with the dispassionate rhythm of sleep.

He listened, that was certain. I listened to his listening. He listened to my listening to his listening. Something snapped. I noticed that I was not thinking at all of what I thought I was thinking; attempted to catch my consciousness tripping, but got mazed myself.

I dreamed a loathsome dream, a triple ephialtes. First there was a small dog; but not simply a small dog; a small mock dog, very small, with the minute black eyes of a beetle's larva; it was white through and through, and coldish. Flesh? No, not flesh, but rather grease or jelly, or else perhaps, the fat of a white worm, with, moreover, a kind of carved corrugated surface reminding one of a Russian paschal lamb of butter—disgusting mimicry. A cold-blooded being, which Nature had twisted into the likeness of a small dog with a tail and legs, all as it should be. It kept getting into my way, I could not avoid it; and when it touched me, I felt something like an electric shock. I woke up. On the sheet of the bed next to mine there lay curled up, like a swooned white larva, that very same dreadful little pseudo dog . . . I groaned with disgust and opened my eyes. All around shadows floated; the bed next to mine was empty except for the broad burdock leaves which, owing to the damp, grow out of bedsteads. One could see, on those leaves, telltale stains of a slimy nature; I peered closer; there, glued to a fat stem it sat, small, tallowish-white, with its little black button eyes . . . but then, at last, I woke up for good.

We had forgotten to pull down the blinds. My wristwatch had stopped. Might be five or half-past five. Felix slept, wrapped up in the feather bed, with his back to me; the dark crown of his head alone was visible. A weird awakening, a weird dawn. I recollected our talk, I remembered that I had not been able to convince him; and a brand-new, most attractive idea got hold of me.

Oh, reader, I felt as fresh as a child after my little snooze; my soul was rinsed clean; I was, in fact, only in my thirty-sixth year, and the generous remainder of my life might be devoted to something better than a vile will-o'-the-wisp. Really, what a fascinating thought; to take the advice of fate and, now, at once, leave that room, forever leave and forget, and spare my poor double. . . . And, who knows, maybe he was not the least like me after all, I could see only the crown of his head, he was fast asleep, with his back to me. Thus an adolescent, after yielding once again to a solitary and shameful vice, says to himself with inordinate force and clearness: "That's finished for good; from this time forth, life shall be pure; the rapture of purity"; thus, after having voiced everything, having lived through everything in advance and had my fill of pain and pleasure, I was now superstitiously keen to turn away from temptation for ever.

All seemed so simple; on that other bed slept a tramp whom I had by chance sheltered; his poor dusty shoes stood on the floor with toes turned in; his trusty stick had been carefully placed across the seat of the chair that supported his clothes folded with proletarian tidiness. What on earth was I doing in that provincial hotel room? What reason was there to loiter? And that sober and heavy smell of a stranger's sweat, that curdled sky in the window, that large black fly settled on the decanter ... all were saying to me: rise and go.

A black smear of gravelly mud on the wall near the switch reminded me of a spring day in Prague. Oh, I could scrape it off so as to leave no trace, no trace, no trace! I longed for the hot bath I would take in my beautiful home—though wryly correcting anticipation with the thought that Ardalion had probably used the tub as his kind cousin had already allowed him to do, I suspected, once or twice in my absence.

I lowered my feet on to an upturned corner of the rug; combed my hair back from the temples with a pocket comb of genuine tortoiseshell—not the dirty mock turtle I had seen that bum using; without a sound, I slipped across the room to put on my overcoat and hat; lifted my suitcase and went out, closing the door noiselessly after me. I presume that had I even happened to cast a glance at the face of my sleeping double, I should have gone all the same; but I experienced no wish to do so, just as the above-mentioned adolescent does not, in the morning, deign to glance at the photograph he had adored in bed.

In a slight haze of dizziness I went down the stairs, polished my shoes with a towel in the lavatory, recombed my hair, paid for the room, and, followed by the night porter's sleepy stare, stepped into the street. Half an hour later I was sitting in a railway carriage; a brandy-flavored belch traveled with me, and in the corners of my mouth lingered the salty traces of a plain, but delicious omelette that I had hurriedly eaten at the station restaurant. Thus, on a low esophageal note, this vague chapter ends.

# Chapter Six

The nonexistence of God is simple to prove. Impossible to concede, for example, that a serious Jah, all wise and almighty, could employ his time in such inane fashion as playing with manikins, and—what is still more incongruous—should restrict his game to the dreadfully trite laws of mechanics, chemistry, mathematics, and never—mind you, never! —show his face, but allow himself surreptitious peeps and circumlocutions, and the sneaky whispering (revelations, indeed!) of contentious truths from behind the back of some gentle hysteric.

All this divine business is, I presume, a huge hoax for which priests are certainly not to blame; priests themselves are its victims. The idea of God was invented in the small hours of history by a scamp who had genius; it somehow reeks too much of humanity, that idea, to make its azure origin plausible; by which I do not mean that it is the fruit of crass ignorance; that scamp of mine was skilled in celestial lore—and really I wonder which variation of Heaven is best: that dazzle of argus-eyed angels fanning their wings, or that curved mirror in which a self-complacent professor of physics recedes, getting ever smaller and smaller. There is yet another reason why I cannot, nor wish to, believe in God: the fairy tale about him is not really mine, it belongs to strangers, to all men; it is soaked through by the evil-smelling effluvia of millions of other souls that have spun about a little under the sun and then burst; it swarms with primordial fears; there echoes in it a confused choir of numberless voices striving to drown one another; I hear in it the boom and pant of the organ, the roar of the orthodox deacon, the croon of the cantor, Negroes wailing, the flowing eloquency of the Protestant preacher, gongs, thunderclaps, spasms of epileptic women; I see shining through it the pallid pages of all philosophies like the foam of long-spent waves; it is foreign to me, and odious and absolutely useless.

If I am not master of my life, not sultan of my own being, then no man's logic and no man's ecstatic fits may force me to find less silly my impossibly silly position: that of God's slave; no, not his slave even, but just a match which is aimlessly struck and then blown out by some inquisitive child, the terror of his toys. There are, however, no grounds for anxiety: God does not exist, as neither does our hereafter, that second bogey being as easily disposed of as the first. Indeed, imagine yourself just dead—and suddenly wide awake in Paradise where, wreathed in smiles, your dear dead welcome you.

Now tell me, please, what guarantee do you possess that those beloved ghosts are genuine; that it is really your dear dead mother and not some petty demon mystifying you, masked as your mother and impersonating her with consummate art and naturalness? There is the rub, there is the horror; the more so as the acting will go on and on, endlessly; never, never, never, never, never will your soul in that other world be quite sure that the sweet gentle spirits crowding about it are not fiends in disguise, and forever, and forever, and forever shall your soul remain in doubt, expecting every moment some awful change, some diabolical sneer to disfigure the dear face bending over you.

That is the reason why I am ready to accept all, come what may; the burly executioner in his top hat, and then the hollow hum of blank eternity; but I refuse to undergo the tortures of everlasting life, I do not want those cold white little dogs. Let me go, I will not stand the least token of tenderness, I warn you, for all is deceit, a low conjuring trick. I do not trust anything or anyone—and when the dearest being I know in this world meets me in the next and the arms I know stretch out to embrace me, I shall emit a yell of sheer horror, I shall collapse on the paradisian turf, writhing ... oh, I know not what I shall do! No, let strangers not be admitted to the land of the blessed.

Still, despite my lack of faith, I am by nature neither sullen nor wicked. When I returned from Tarnitz to Berlin and drew up an inventory of my soul's belongings, I rejoiced like a child over the small but certain riches found therein, and I had the sensation that, renovated, refreshed, released, I was entering, as the saying goes, upon a new period of life. I had a bird-witted but attractive wife who worshiped me; a nice little flat; an accommodating stomach; and a blue car. There was in me, I felt, a poet, an author; also, big commercial capacities, albeit business remained pretty dull. Felix, my double, seemed no more than a harmless curio, and, quite possibly, I should in those days have told friends about him, had I had any friends. I toyed with the idea of dropping my chocolate and taking up something else; the publishing, for instance, of expensive volumes *de luxe* dealing exhaustively with sexual relations as revealed in literature, art, science ... in short, I was bursting with fierce energy which I did not know how to apply.

One November evening, especially, stands out in my memory: upon coming home from the office I did not find my wife in—she had left me a note saying she had gone to the movies. Not knowing what to do with myself I paced the rooms and snapped my fingers; then sat down at my desk with the intention of writing a bit of fine prose, but all I managed to do was to beslobber my pen and draw a series of running noses; so I got up and went out, because I was in sore need of some sort—any sort of intercourse with the world, my own company being intolerable, since it excited me too much and to no purpose. I betook myself to Ardalion; a mountebank of a man, red-blooded and despicable. When at last he let me in (he locked himself up in his room for fear of creditors) I caught myself wondering why had I come at all.

"Lydia is here," he said, revolving something in his mouth (chewing gum as it proved later). "The woman is very ill. Make yourself comfortable."

On Ardalion's bed, half dressed—that is, shoeless and wearing only a rumpled green slip—Lydia lay smoking.

"Oh, Hermann," she said, "how nice of you to think of coming. There's something wrong with my tum. Sit down here. It's better now, but I felt awful at the cinema."

"In the middle of a jolly good film, too," Ardalion complained, as he poked at his pipe and scattered its black contents about the floor. "She's been sprawling like that for the last half hour. A woman's imagination, that's all. Fit as a fiddle."

"Tell him to hold his tongue," said Lydia.

"Look here," I said, turning to Ardalion, "surely I am not mistaken; you have painted, haven't you, such a picture —a briar pipe and two roses?"

He produced a sound, which indiscriminate novel-writers render thus: "H'm."

"Not that I know of," he replied, "you seem to have been working too much, old chap."

"My first," said Lydia lying on the bed, with her eyes shut, "my first is a romantic fiery feeling. My second is a beast. My whole is a beast too, if you like—or else a dauber."

"Do not mind her," said Ardalion. "As to that pipe and roses, no, I can't think of it. But you might look for yourself."

His daubs hung on the walls, lay in disorder on the table, were heaped in a corner. Everything in the room was fluffy with dust. I examined the smudgy purplish spots of his water colors; fingered gingerly several greasy pastels lying on a rickety chair...

"First," said Ardor-lion to his fair cousin, a horrid tease, "you should learn to spell my name."

I left the room and made my way to the landlady's dining room. That ancient dame, very like an owl, was sitting in a Gothic armchair which stood on a slight elevation of the floor next to the window and was darning a stocking distended upon a wooden mushroom.

"... To see the pictures," I said.

"Pray do," she answered graciously.

Immediately to the right of the sideboard I espied what I was seeking; it turned out, however, to be not quite two roses and not quite a pipe, but a couple of large peaches and a glass ashtray.

I came back in a state of acute irritation.

"Well," Ardalion inquired, "found it?"

Shook my head. Lydia had already slipped on her dress

and shoes and was in the act of smoothing her hair before
the mirror with Ardalion's hairbrush.

"Funny—must have eaten something," she said with that
little trick she had of narrowing her nose.

"Just wind," remarked Ardalion. "Wait a moment, you
people. I'm coming with you. I'll be dressed in a jiffy. Turn
away, Lyddy."

He was in a patched, color-smeared house-painter's smock,
coming down almost to his heels. This he took off. There
was nothing beneath save his silver cross and symmetrical
tufts of hair. I do hate slovenliness and dirt. Upon my word,
Felix was somehow cleaner than he. Lydia looked out of the
window and kept humming a little song which had long gone
out of fashion (and how badly she pronounced the German
words). Ardalion wandered about the room, dressing by
stages according to what he discovered in the most unexpected spots.

"Ah, me!" he exclaimed all at once. "What can there be
more commonplace than an impecunious artist? If some good
soul helped me to arrange an exhibition, next day I'd be
famous and rich."

He had supper with us, then played cards with Lydia and
left after midnight. I offer all this as a sample of an evening
gaily and profitably spent. Yes, all was well, all was excellent,
I felt another man, refreshed, renovated, released (a flat, a
wife, the pleasant, all-pervading cold of an iron-hard Berlin
winter) and so on. I cannot refrain from giving as well an
instance of my literary exercises—a sort of subconscious train-
ing, I suppose, in view of my present tussle with this harass-
ing tale. The coy trifles composed that winter have been
destroyed, but one of them still lingers in my memory. . . .
Which reminds me of Turgenev's prose-poems. . . . "How fair,

how fresh were the roses" to the accompaniment of the piano. So may I trouble you for a little music.

Once upon a time there lived a weak, seedy, but fairly rich person, one Mr. X.Y. He was in love with a bewitching young lady, who, alas, paid no attention to him. One day, while traveling, this pale, dull man happened to notice, on the seashore, a young fisherman called Mario, a merry, sun-burned, strong fellow, who, for all that, was marvelously, stupendously like him. A cute idea occurred to our hero: he invited the young lady to come with him to the seaside. They lodged at different hotels. On the very first morning she went for a walk and saw from the top of the cliff—whom? Was that really Mr. X.Y.? Well, I never! He was standing on the sand below, merry, sunburnt, in a striped jersey, with bare strong arms (but it was Mario!). The damsel returned to her hotel all aquiver and waited, waited! The golden minutes turning into lead . . .

In the meantime the real Mr. X.Y. who, from behind a bay tree, had seen her looking down at Mario, his double (and was now giving her heart time to ripen definitely), loitered anxiously about the village dressed in a town suit, with a lilac tie. All of a sudden a brown fishergirl in a scarlet skirt called out to him from the threshold of a cottage and with a Latin gesture of surprise exclaimed: "How wonderfully you are dressed up, Mario! I always thought you were a simple rude fisherman, as all our young men are, and I did not love you; but now, now . . ." She drew him into the hut. Whisper-ing lips, a blend of fish and hair lotion, burning caresses. So the hours fled. . . .

At last Mr. X.Y. opened his eyes and went to the hotel where his dear one, his only love, was feverishly awaiting him. "I have been blind," she cried as he entered. "And now my sight has been restored by your appearing in all your bronze nakedness on that sun-kissed beach. Yes, I love you. Do with me what you will." Whispering lips? Burning caresses? Fleeting hours? No, alas, no—emphatically no. Only a lingering smell of fish. The poor fellow was thoroughly spent by his recent spree, and so there he sat, very glum and downcast, thinking what a fool he had been to betray and annul his own glorious plan.

Very mediocre stuff, I know that myself. During the process of writing I was under the impression that I was turning out something very smart and witty; on occasions a like thing happens in dreams: you dream you are making a speech of the utmost brilliancy, but when you recall it upon awakening, it goes nonsensically: "Besides being silent before tea, I'm silent before eyes in mire and mirorage," etc.

On the other hand, that little story in the Oscar Wilde style would quite suit the literary columns of newspapers, the editors of which, German editors especially, like to offer their readers just such tiny tales of the pretty-pretty and slightly licentious sort, forty lines in all, with an elegant point and a sprinkling of what the ignoramus calls paradoxes ("his conversation sparkled with paradoxes"). Yes, a trifle, a flip of the pen, but how amazed you will be when I tell you that I wrote that soppy drivel in an agony of pain and horror, with a grinding of teeth, furiously unburdening myself and at the same time being fully aware that it was no relief at all, only a refined self-torture, and that I would never free my dusty, dusky soul by this method, but merely make things worse.

It was more or less in such a frame of mind that I met New Year's Eve; I remember the black carcass of that night, that half-witted hag of a night, holding her breath and listening for the stroke of the sacramental hour. Disclosed, sitting at the table: Lydia, Ardalion, Orlovius, and I, quite still and blazon-stiff like heraldic creatures. Lydia with her elbow on the table, her index finger raised watchfully, her shoulders naked, her dress as variegated as the back of a playing card; Ardalion swathed in a laprobe (because of the open balcony door), with a red sheen upon his fat leonine face; Orlovius in a black frock coat, his glasses gleaming, his turned-down collar swallowing the ends of his tiny black tie; and I, the Human Lightning, illuminating that scene.

Good, now you may move again, be quick with that bottle, the clock is going to strike. Ardalion poured out the champagne, and we were all dead-still once more. Askance and over his spectacles, Orlovius looked at his old silver turnip that lay on the tablecloth; still two minutes left. Somebody in the street was unable to hold out any longer and cracked with a loud report; and then again that strained silence. Staring at his watch, Orlovius slowly extended toward his glass a senile hand with the claws of a griffin.

Suddenly the night gave and began to rip; cheers came from the street; with our champagne glasses we came out, like kings, on the balcony. Rockets whizzed up above the street and with a bang burst into bright-colored tears; and at all windows, on all balconies, framed in wedges and squares of festive light, people stood and cried out over and over again the same idiotic greeting.

We four clinked our glasses; I took a sip out of mine.

"What is Hermann drinking to?" asked Lydia of Ardalion.

"Don't know and don't care," the latter replied. "Whatever it is, he is going to be beheaded this year. For concealing his profits."

"Fie, what ugly speech!" said Orlovius. "I drink to the universal health."

"You would," I remarked.

A few days later, on a Sunday morning, as I was about to step into my bath, the maid rapped at the door; she kept saying something which I could not distinguish because of the running water: "What's the matter?" I bellowed. "What d'you want?"—but my own voice and the noise made by the water drowned Elsie's words and every time she started speaking, I again bellowed, just as it happens that two people, both side-stepping, cannot steer clear of each other on a wide and perfectly free pavement. But at length I thought of turning off the tap; then I leaped to the door and amid the sudden silence Elsie's childish voice said:

"There's a man, sir, to see you."

"A man?" I asked, and opened the door.

"A man," repeated Elsie, as if commenting on my nakedness.

"What does he want?" I asked, and not only felt myself perspiring but actually *saw* myself beaded from head to foot.

"He says it's business, sir, and you know all about it."

"What does he look like?" I asked with an effort.

"Waiting in the hall," said Elsie, contemplating with the utmost indifference my pearly armor.

"What kind of man?"

"Kind of poor, sir, and with a shoulder bag."

"Then tell him to go to hell!" I roared. "Let him be gone at once, I'm not at home, I'm not in town, I'm not in this world."

I slammed the door, shot the bolt. My heart seemed to be pounding right up in my throat. Half a minute or so passed. I do not know what came over me, but, already shouting, I suddenly unfastened the door and still naked, jumped out of the bathroom. In the passage I collided with Elsie who was returning to the kitchen.

"Stop him," I shouted. "Where is he? Stop him."

"He's gone," she said, politely disengaging herself from my unintentional embrace.

"Why the deuce did you—" I began, but did not finish my sentence, rushed away, put on shoes, trousers and overcoat, ran downstairs and out into the street. Nobody. I went on to the corner, stood there for a while looking about me and finally went back indoors. I was alone, as Lydia had gone out very early to see some female acquaintance of hers, she said. When she returned I told her I was feeling out of sorts and would not come with her to the café as had been settled.

"Poor thing," she said. "You should lie down and take something; there's aspirin somewhere. All right. I'll go to the café alone."

She went. The maid had gone out too. I listened in agony for the doorbell to ring.

"What a fool," I kept repeating, "what an incredible fool!"

I was in an awful state of quite morbid exasperation. I did not know what to do, I was ready to pray to a nonexistent God for the sound of the bell. When it grew dark I did not switch on the light, but remained lying on the divan—listening, listening. He was sure to come before the front door was locked for the night, and if he did not, well, then tomorrow, or the day after tomorrow he was quite, quite certain to come. I should die if he did not—oh, he was bound to come. . . . At last, about eight o'clock the bell did ring. I ran to the door.

"Phew, I *am* tired!" said Lydia in homely fashion, pulling her hat off as she entered, and tossing her hair.

She was accompanied by Ardalion. He and I went to the parlor, while my wife got busy in the kitchen.

"Cold is the pilgrim and hungry!" said Ardalion, warming his palms at the central heating and misquoting the poet Nekrasov.

A silence.

"Say what you may," he went on, peering at my portrait, "but there *is* a likeness, quite a remarkable likeness, in fact. I know I'm being conceited, but, really, I can't help admiring it every blessed time I see it. And you've done well, my dear fellow, to shave that mustache off again."

"Supper is served," chanted Lydia gently, from the dining room.

I could not touch my food. I kept on sending one ear out to walk up and again up to the door of my flat, though it was much too late now.

"Two pet dreams of mine," spoke Ardalion, folding up layers of ham as if it were pancakes, and richly munching. "Two heavenly dreams: exhibition and trip to Italy."

"This person has not touched a drop of vodka for more than a month," said Lydia in an explanatory way.

"Talking of vodka," said Ardalion, "has Perebrodov been to see you?"

Lydia put her hand to her mouth. " 'Scaped by bebory," she said through her fingers. "Absolutely."

"Never saw such a goose. The fact is I had asked her to tell you . . . It's about a poor artist-fellow—Perebrodov by name—old pal of mine and all that. Came on foot from Danzig you know, or at least says he did. He sells hand-painted cigarette-cases, so I gave him your address—Lydia, thought you'd help him."

"Oh, yes, he has called," I answered, "yes, he has called

all right. And I jolly well told him to go to the devil. I'd be most obliged to you, if you'd stop sending me all kinds of sponging rogues. You may tell your friend not to bother about coming again. Really—it's a bit thick. Anyone would think I was a professional benefactor. Go to blazes with your what's-his-name—I simply won't have..."

"There, there, Hermann," put in Lydia softly.

Ardalion made an explosive sound with his lips. "Passing sad," he observed.

I went on fuming for some time—don't remember the exact words—not important.

"It really seems," said Ardalion with a side glance at Lydia, "I have put my foot in. Sorry."

I fell silent suddenly and sat deep in thought, stirring my tea which had long done all it could with the sugar; then after a time I said aloud:

"What a perfect donkey I am."

"Oh, come, don't overdo it," said Ardalion good-naturedly.

My own folly made me gay. How on earth had it not occurred to me that if Felix had actually come (which in itself would have been something of a wonder, considering he did not even know my name), the maid ought to have been flabbergasted, for in front of her would have stood my perfect double!

Now that I had come to think of it my fancy conjured up vividly the girl's ejaculation, and how she would have rushed to me and gasped, and clung to me, babbling about the marvel of our resemblance. Then I would have explained to her that it was my brother unexpectedly arrived from Russia. As it was I had spent a long lonely day in absurd sufferings, for instead of being surprised by the bare fact of

[ 113 ]

his coming I had kept trying to decide what was going to happen next—whether he had gone for good or would come back yet, and what was his game, and had not his coming vitiated the fulfillment of my still unvanquished, wild and wonderful dream; or alternatively, had a score of people, knowing my face, seen him in the street, which, if so, would have meant an end to my plans.

After having thus pondered over the shortcomings of my reason, and the danger so easily dispelled, I felt, as already mentioned, a flow of merriment and good will.

"I'm nervy today. Please excuse me. To be honest, I have simply not seen your delightful friend. He came at the wrong moment. I was having my bath, and Elsie told him I wasn't in. Here: give him these three marks when you see him—what I can do I do gladly—and tell him I can't afford any more, so he'd better apply to somebody else—to Vladimir Isakovich Davidov, perhaps."

"That's an idea," said Ardalion, "I'll have a shot there myself. By the bye, he drinks like a fish, good old Perebrodov. Ask that aunt of mine, who married a French farmer—I told you about her—a very lively lady, but dashed close-fisted. She had some land in the Crimea and during the fighting there in 1920 Perebrodov and I drank up her cellar."

"As to that trip to Italy—well, we shall see," said I, smiling, "yes, we shall see."

"Hermann has a heart of gold," remarked Lydia.

"Pass me the sausage, my dear," said I, smiling as before.

I could not quite make out at the time what was going on in me—but now I know what it was: my passion for my double was surging anew with a muffled but formidable violence which soon escaped all control. It started by my becoming aware that, in the town of Berlin, there had appeared a certain dim central point round which a confused force compelled me to circle closer and closer. The cobalt blue of mailboxes, or that yellow plump-wheeled automobile with the emblematic black-feathered eagle under its barred window; a postman with his bag on his belly walking down the street (with that special rich slowness which marks the ways of the experienced worker) or the stamp-emitting automaton at the underground station; or even some little philatelistic shop, with appetizingly blended stamps from all parts of the world crammed into windowed envelopes; in short, everything connected with the post had begun to exercise upon me a strange pressure, a ruthless influence.

I remember that one day something very like somnambulism took me to a certain lane I knew well, and so there I was, moving nearer and nearer to the magnetic point that had become the peg of my being; but with a start I collected my wits and fled; and presently—within a few minutes or quite as possibly within a few days—I noticed that again I had entered that lane. It was distribution time, and they came toward me, at a leisurely walk, a dozen blue postmen, and leisurely they dispersed at the corner. I turned, biting my thumb, I shook my head, I was still resisting; and all the while, with the mad throb of unerring intuition, I knew that the letter was there, awaiting my call and that sooner or later I would yield to temptation.

# Chapter Seven

To begin with, let us take the following motto (not especially for this chapter, but generally): Literature is Love. Now we can continue.

It was darkish in the post office; two or three people stood at every counter, mostly women; and at every counter, framed in his little window, like some tarnished picture, showed the face of an official. I looked for number nine. . . . I wavered before going up to it. . . . There was, in the middle of the place, a series of writing desks, so I lingered there, pretending, in front of my own self, that I had something to write: on the back of an old bill which I found in my pocket, I began to scrawl the very first words that came. The pen supplied by the State screeched and rattled, I kept thrusting it into the inkwell, into the black spit therein; the pale blotting paper upon which I leaned my elbow was all criss-crossed with the imprints of unreadable lines. Those irrational characters, preceded as it were by a minus, remind me always of mirrors: minus $\times$ minus $=$ plus. It struck me that perhaps Felix too was a minus I, and that was a line of thought of quite astounding importance, which I did wrong, oh, very wrong, not to have thoroughly investigated.

Meanwhile the consumptive pen in my hand went on spitting words: can't stop, can't stop, cans, pots, stop, he'll to

hell. I crumpled the slip of paper in my fist. An impatient
fat female squeezed in and snatched up the pen, now free,
shoving me aside as she did so with a twist of her sealskin
rump.

All of a sudden I found myself standing at counter nine.
A large face with a sandy moustache glanced at me inquir-
ingly. I breathed the password. A hand with a black cot on
the index finger gave me not one but three letters. It now
seems to me to have all happened in a flash; and the next
moment I was walking along the street with my hand pressed
to my heart. As soon as I reached a bench I sat down and
tore the letters open.

Put up some memorial there; for instance, a yellow signpost. Let that particle of time leave a mark in space as well.
There I was, sitting and reading—and then suddenly choking
with unexpected and irrepressible laughter. Oh, courteous
reader, those were letters of the blackmailing kind! A blackmailing letter, which none perhaps will ever unseal, a blackmailing letter addressed P.O. till called for, under an agreed
cipher, to boot, i.e., with the candid confession that its sender
knows neither the name nor the address of the person he
writes to—that is a wildly funny paradox indeed!

In the first of those three letters (middle of November)
the blackmail theme was merely foreshadowed. It was much
offended with me, that letter, it demanded explanations, it
seemed verily to elevate its eyebrows, as its author did, ready
at a moment's notice to smile his arch smile; for he did not
understand, he said, he was extremely desirous to understand,
why I had behaved so mysteriously, why I had, without
clinching matters, stolen away in the dead of night. He did
have certain suspicions, that he did, but was not willing to
show his cards yet; was ready to conceal those suspicions from

the world, if only I acted as I should; and with dignity he expressed his hesitations and with dignity expected a reply. It was all very ungrammatical and, at the same time stilted, that mixture being his natural style.

In the next letter (end of December. What patience!) the specific theme was already more conspicuous. It was plain now why he wrote to me at all. The memory of that one-thousand-mark note, of that grey-blue vision which had whisked under his very nose and then vanished, gnawed at his entrails; his cupidity was stung to the quick, he licked his parched lips, he could not forgive himself for having let me go and thus been cheated of that adorable rustle, which made the tips of his fingers itch. So he wrote that he was ready to grant me a new interview; that he had thought things over of late; but that if I declined seeing him or simply did not reply he would be compelled—right here came pat an enormous ink-blot which the scoundrel had made on purpose with the object of intriguing me, as he had not the faintest notion what kind of threat to declare.

Lastly, the third, January, letter was a true masterpiece on his part. I remember it in more detail than the rest, because I preserved it somewhat longer:

Receiving no answers to my first letters it begins seeming to me that it is high time to adopt certain measures but notwithstanding I give you one more month for reflection after which I shall go straight to such a place where your actions will be fully judged at their full value though if there also I find no sympathy for who is uncorruptible nowadays then I shall have recourse to action the exact nature of which I leave wholly to your imagination as I consider that when the government does not want and there is an end of it to punish swindlers it is every honest citizen's duty to produce such a crashing din in relation to the undesirable person as to make the state react willy-nilly but in view of your personal situation and from considerations of kindness and readiness to oblige I am prepared to give up my intention and refrain from making any noise upon the condition that during the current month you send me please a rather considerable sum as indemnity for all the worries I have had the exact amount of which I leave with respect to your own estimation.

Signed: "Sparrow" and underneath the address of a provincial post office.

I was long in relishing that last letter, the Gothic charm of which my rather tame translation is hardly capable of rendering. All its features pleased me: that majestic stream of words, untrammeled by a single punctuation mark; that doltish display of puny curdom coming from so harmless-looking an individual; that implied consent to accept any proposal, however revolting, provided he got the money. But what, above all, gave me delight, delight of such force and ripeness that it was difficult to bear, consisted in the fact that Felix of his own accord, without any prompting from me, had reappeared and was offering me his services; nay, more: was commanding me to make use of his services and, withal doing everything I wished, was relieving me of any responsibility that might be incurred by the fatal succession of events.

I rocked with laughter as I sat on that bench. Oh, do erect a monument there (a yellow post) by all means! How did he conceive it—the simpleton? That his letters would, by some sort of telepathy, inform me of their arrival and that after a magical perusal of their contents I would magically believe in the potency of his phantom menaces? How amusing that I *did* somehow feel that the letters awaited me, counter num-

ber nine, and that I *did* intend answering them, in other
words, what he—in his arrogant stupidity—had conjectured,
*had* happened!

As I sat on that bench and clasped those letters in my
burning embrace, I was suddenly aware that my scheme had
received a final outline and that everything, or nearly everything, was already settled; a mere couple of details were still
missing which would be no trouble to fix. What, indeed, does
trouble mean in such matters? It all went on by itself, it all
flowed and fused together, smoothly taking inevitable forms,
since that very moment when I had first seen Felix.

Why, what is this talk about trouble, when it is the harmony of mathematical symbols, the movement of planets, the
hitchless working of natural laws which have a true bearing
upon the subject? My wonderful edifice grew without my
assistance; yes, from the very start everything had complied
with my wishes; and when now I asked myself what to write
to Felix, I was hardly astonished to find that letter in my
brain, as ready-made there as those congratulatory telegrams
with vignettes that can be sent for a certain additional payment to newly married couples. It only remained to inscribe
the date in the space left for it on the printed form.

Let us discuss crime, crime as an art; and card tricks. I am
greatly worked up just at present. Oh, Conan Doyle! How
marvelously you could have crowned your creation when
your two heroes began boring you! What an opportunity,
what a subject you missed! For you could have written one
last tale concluding the whole Sherlock Holmes epic; one
last episode beautifully setting off the rest: the murderer in
that tale should have turned out to be not the one-legged
bookkeeper, not the Chinaman Ching and not the woman
in crimson, but the very chronicler of the crime stories, Dr.

Watson himself—Watson, who, so to speak, knew what was Whatson. A staggering surprise for the reader.

But what are they—Doyle, Dostoevsky, Leblanc, Wallace—what are all the great novelists who wrote of nimble criminals, what are all the great criminals who never read the nimble novelists—what are they in comparison with me? Blundering fools! As in the case of inventive geniuses, I was certainly helped by chance (my meeting Felix), but that piece of luck fitted exactly into the place I had made for it; I pounced upon it and used it, which another in my position would not have done.

My accomplishment resembles a game of patience, arranged beforehand; first I put down the open cards in such a manner as to make its success a dead certainty; then I gathered them up in the opposite order and gave the prepared pack to others with the perfect assurance it would come out.

The mistake of my innumerable forerunners consisted of their laying principal stress upon the act itself and in their attaching more importance to a subsequent removal of all traces, than to the most natural way of leading up to that same act which is really but a link in the chain, one detail, one line in the book, and must be logically derived from all previous matter; such being the nature of every art. If the deed is planned and performed correctly, then the force of creative art is such, that were the criminal to give himself up on the very next morning, none would believe him, the invention of art containing far more intrinsical truth than life's reality.

All this, I remember, sped through my mind, just at the time I was sitting with those letters in my lap, but then it was one thing, now another; *now* I would slightly amend the statement, adding to it that (as happens with wonderful works of art which the mob refuses, for a long time, to understand, to acknowledge, and the spell of which it resists) the genius of a perfect crime is not admitted by people and does not make them dream and wonder; instead, they do their best to pick out something that can be pecked at and pulled to bits, something to prod the author with, so as to hurt him as much as possible. And when they think they have discovered the lapse they are after, hear their guffaws and jeers! But it is they who have erred, not the author; they lack his keensightedness and see nothing out of the common there, where the author perceived a marvel.

After having laughed my fill and then quietly and clearly thought out my next moves, I put the third and most vicious letter into my pocketbook and tore up the other two, throwing their fragments into the neighboring shrubbery (which at once attracted several sparrows who mistook them for crumbs). Then I sallied to my office where I typed a letter to Felix with detailed indications as to when and where he should come; enclosed twenty marks and went out again.

I have always found it difficult to loosen my grip of the letter suspended above the abysmal chink. It is like diving into icy water or jumping from a burning balcony into what looks like the heart of an artichoke, and now it was particularly hard to let go. I gulped, I felt a queer sinking in the pit of my stomach; and still holding the letter, I proceeded down the street and stopped at the next letter box, where the same thing happened all over again. I walked on, burdened by the letter and fairly bending under that huge white load, and again, beyond a block of houses, I came to a letter box. My indecision was becoming a nuisance, as it was quite causeless and senseless in view of the firmness of my intentions; perhaps it could be dismissed as a physical, mechanical indecision, a muscular reluctance to relax; or, better still, it might be, as a Marxist observer would put it (Marxism getting the nearest to Absolute Truth, as I always say)—the indecision of an owner who is always loath (such being his very essence) to part with property; and it is noteworthy that in my case the idea of property was not confined merely to the money I was sending, but corresponded to that share of my soul which I had put into my letter. Be it as it might, I had already overcome my hesitation when I reached my fourth or fifth letter box. I knew as distinctly as I know that I am going to set down this sentence—I knew that nothing could prevent me from dropping now the letter into the slit, and I even foresaw the sort of little gesture I would make immediately afterwards—brushing one palm against the other, as if some specks of dust had been left on my gloves by the letter, which, being posted, was mine no more, and so its dust was not mine either. That's done, that's finished (such was the meaning of my imagined gesture).

Nevertheless, I did not drop the letter in, but stood there, bending under my burden as before, and looking from under my brows at two little girls playing near me on the pavement: they rolled by turns an iridescent marble, aiming at a pit in the soil near the curb.

I selected the younger of the two—she was a delicate little thing, dark-haired, dressed in a checkered frock (what a wonder she was not cold on that harsh February day) and, patting her on the head, I said: "Look here, my dear, my eyes are so weak that I'm afraid of missing the slit; do, please, drop this letter for me into the box over there."

She glanced up at me, rose from her squatting position (she had a small face of translucent pallor and rare beauty), took the letter, gave me a divine smile accompanied by a sweep of her long lashes, and ran to the letter box. I did not wait to see the rest, and crossed the street, slitting my eyes (that ought to be noted) as if I really did not see well: art for art's sake, for there was no one about.

At the next corner I slipped into the glass booth of a public telephone and rang up Ardalion: it was necessary to do something about him as I had decided long ago that this meddlesome portrait-painter was the only person of whom I ought to beware. Let psychologists clear up the question whether it was the simulation of nearsightedness that by association prompted me to act at once toward Ardalion as I had long intended to act, or was it, on the contrary, my constantly reminding myself of his dangerous eyes that gave me the idea of feigning nearsightedness.

Oh, by the bye, lest I forget, she will grow up, that child, she will be very good-looking and probably happy, and she will never know in what an eerie business she had served as go-between.

Then, also, there is another likelihood: fate, not suffering such blind and naïve brokerage, envious fate with its vast experience, assortment of confidence tricks, and hatred of competition, may cruelly punish that little maiden for intruding, and make her wonder— "Whatever have I done to be so unfortunate?" and never, never, never will she understand. But *my* conscience is clear. Not I wrote to Felix, but he wrote to me; not I sent him the answer, but an unknown child.

When I reached my next destination, a pleasant café, in front of which, amid a small public garden, there used to play on summer evenings a fountain of changing colors, cleverly lit up from below by polychromatic projectors (but now the garden was bare and dreary, and no fountain twinkled, and the thick curtains of the café had won in their class struggle with loafing draughts . . . how racily I write and, what is more, how cool I am, how perfectly self-possessed); when, as I say, I arrived, Ardalion was already sitting there, and upon seeing me, he raised his arm in the Roman fashion. I took off my gloves, my hat, my white silk muffler, sat down next to him, and threw out on the table a packet of expensive cigarettes.

"What are the good tidings?" asked Ardalion, who always spoke to me in a special fatuous manner.

I ordered coffee and began approximately thus:

"Well, yes—there *is* news for you. Of late I have been greatly worried, my friend, by the thought that you were going to the dogs. An artist cannot live without mistresses and cypresses, as Pushkin says somewhere or should have said. Owing to the hardships you undergo and to the general stuffiness of your way of living, your talent is dying, is pining away, so to speak; does not squirt in fact, just as that colored fountain in that garden over there does not squirt in winter."

"Thank you for the comparison," said Ardalion, looking hurt. "That horror . . . that illumination in the caramel style. I would rather, you know, not discuss my talent, because your conception of *ars pictoris* amounts to . . ." (an unprintable pun here).

"Lydia and I have often spoken," I went on, ignoring his dog-latin and vulgarity—"spoken about your plight. I consider you ought to change your surroundings, refresh your mind, imbibe new impressions."

Ardalion winced.

"What have surroundings to do with art?" he muttered.

"Anyway, your present ones are disastrous to you, so they do mean something, I suppose. Those roses and peaches with which you adorn your landlady's dining room, those portraits of respectable citizens at whose houses you contrive to sup—"

"Well, really . . . contrive!"

". . . It may all be admirable, even full of genius, but—excuse my frankness—doesn't it strike you as rather monotonous and forced? You ought to dwell in some other clime with plenty of sunshine: sunshine is the friend of painters. I can see, though, that this topic doesn't interest you. Let's talk of something else. Tell me, for instance, how do matters stand with that allotment of yours?"

"Dashed if I know. They keep sending me letters in German; I'd ask you for a translation, but it bores me stiff. . . . And—well, I either lose the things or just tear them up as they come. I understand they demand additional payments. Next summer I'll build a house there, that's what I'll do. Then they won't pull out the land from under it, I fancy. But you were speaking, my dear chap, about a change of climate. Go on, I'm listening."

"Oh, it's not much use, you are not interested. I talk sense and that nettles you."

"God bless you, why on earth should I be nettled? On the contrary—"

"No, it's no use."

"You mentioned Italy, my dear chap. Fire away. I like the subject."

"I haven't really mentioned it yet," said I with a laugh. "But as *you* have pronounced that word . . . I say, isn't it nice and cosy here? There are rumors that you have stopped . . ." —and by a succession of fillips under my jaw I produced the sound of a gurgling bottleneck.

"Yes. Cut out drink altogether. I'd not refuse one just now, though. The cracking-a-bottle-with-a-friend affair, if you see what I mean. Oh, all right, I was only joking. . . ."

"So much the better, because nothing would come of it: quite impossible to make me tight. So that's that. Heigh-ho, how badly I have slept tonight! Heigh-ho . . . ah! Awful thing insomnia," I went on, looking at him through my tears. "Ah. . . . Do pardon me for yawning like that."

Ardalion, smiling wistfully, was toying with his spoon. His fat face, with its leonine nose-bridge, was inclined; his eyelids —reddish warts for lashes—half screened his revoltingly bright eyes. All of a sudden he flashed a glance at me and said:

"If I took a trip to Italy, I'd indeed paint some gorgeous stuff. What I'd get out of selling it, would at once go to settle my debt."

"Your debt? Got debts?" I asked mockingly.

"Oh, drop it, Hermann Karlovich," said he, using for the first time, I think, my name and patronymic. "You quite understand what I'm driving at. Lend me two hundred fifty marks, or make it dollars, and I'll pray for your soul in all the Florentine churches."

"For the moment take this to pay for your visa," said I flinging open my wallet. "You have, I suppose, one of those Nansen-sical passports, not a solid German one, as all decent people have. Ask for the visa immediately, otherwise you'll spend this advance on drink."

"Shake hands, old man," said Ardalion.

We both kept silent awhile, he, because he was brimming with feelings, which meant little to me, and I, because the matter was ended and there was nothing to say.

"Brilliant idea," cried Ardalion suddenly. "My dear chap, why shouldn't you let Lyddy come with me; it's damn dull here; the little woman needs something to amuse her. Now if I go by myself . . . You see she's of the jealous sort—she'll keep imagining me getting tight somewhere. Really, do let her come away with me for a month, eh?"

"Maybe she'll come later on. Maybe we'll both come. Long have I, weary slave, been planning my escape to the far land of art and the translucent grape. Good. I'm afraid I've got to go now. Two coffees; that's all, isn't it?"

# Chapter Eight

Early next morning—it was not nine yet—I made my way to
one of the central underground stations and there, at the top
of the stairs, took up a strategical position. At even intervals
there would come rushing out of the cavernous deep a batch
of people with briefcases—up, up the stairs, shuffling and
stamping, and every now and again somebody's toe would
hit, with a clank, the metallic advertisement sign which a
certain firm finds it advisable to affix to the front part of the
steps. On the second one from the top, with his back to the
wall and his hat in his hand (who was the first mendicant
genius who adapted a hat to the wants of his profession?),
there stood, stooping his shoulders as humbly as possible, an
elderly wretch. Higher still, there was an assembly of newspaper vendors with coxcomb caps and all hung about with
posters. It was a dark, miserable day; in spite of my wearing
spats, my feet were numb with cold. I wondered if perhaps
they would freeze less if I did not give my black shoes such
a smart shine: a passing and repassing thought. At last,
punctually at five minutes to nine, just as I had reckoned,
Orlovius's figure appeared from the deep. I at once turned
and walked slowly away; Orlovius outstrode me, glanced
back and exposed his fine but false teeth. Our meeting had
the exact color of chance I wanted.

"Yes, I'm coming your way," said I in answer to his question. "I've got to visit my bank."

"Dog's weather," said Orlovius floundering at my side. "How is your wife? Very well?"

"Thanks, she is all right."

"And how are you going on? Not very well?" he continued to inquire courteously.

"No, not very. Nerves, insomnia. Trifles that would have amused me before now annoy me."

"Consume lemons," put in Orlovius.

". . . . that would have amused me before now annoy me. Here, for instance—"

I gave a slight snort of laughter, and produced my pocket-book. "I got this idiotic blackmailing letter, and it somehow weighs upon my mind. Read it if you like, it's a rum business."

Orlovius stopped and scrutinized the letter closely. While he read, I examined the shop window near which we were standing: there, pompous and inane, a couple of bathtubs and various other lavatory accessories gleamed white; and next to it was a shop window with coffins and there, too, all looked pompous and silly.

"Tut-tut," uttered Orlovius. "Do you know who has been writing this?"

I popped the letter back into my wallet and replied with a snigger:

"Of course I do. A rogue. He was at one time in the service of a distant relation of mine. An abnormal creature, if not frankly insane. Got it into his head my family had deprived him of some inheritance; you know how it is: a fixed conviction which nothing can shatter."

Orlovius explained to me, with copious details, the danger

lunatics present to the community and then inquired whether I was going to inform the police.

I shrugged my shoulders: "Nonsense.... Not worth really discussing.... Tell me, what do you think of the Chancellor's speech—read it?"

We continued to walk side by side, comfortably conversing about foreign and home politics. At the door of his office I started removing—as the rules of Russian politeness request— the glove from the hand I was going to proffer.

"It is bad that you are so nervous," said Orlovius. "I pray you, greet, please, your wife."

"I shall do so by all means. Only you know, I am pretty envious of your bachelorhood."

"Why so?"

"It's like this. Hurts me to speak of it, but, you see, my married life is not happy. My wife has a fickle heart, and— well, she's interested in somebody else. Yes, cold and frivolous, that's what I call her, and I don't think she'd weep long if I happened ... er ... you know what I mean. And do forgive me for airing such intimate troubles."

"Certain things I have long observed," said Orlovius nodding his head sagely and sadly.

I shook his woolen paw and we parted. It had all worked beautifully. Old birds like Orlovius are wonderfully easy to lead by the beak, because a combination of decency and sentimentality is exactly equal to being a fool. In his eagerness to sympathize with everybody, not only did he take sides with the noble loving husband when I slandered my exemplary wife, but even decided privately that he had "long observed" (as he put it) a thing or two. I would give a lot to know what that purblind eagle could detect in the cloudless blue of our wedlock. Yes, it had all worked beautifully. I was satisfied.

I would have been still more satisfied had there not been some miscarriage about the getting of that Italian visa.

Ardalion, with Lydia's help, filled out the application form, after which he was told that at least a fortnight would elapse till the visa could be granted (I had about one month before me till the ninth of March; in the worst case, I could always write to Felix changing the date). At last, late in February, Ardalion received his visa and bought his ticket. Moreover, I gave him a thousand marks—it would last him, I hoped, two or three months. He had arranged to go on the first of March, but it transpired suddenly that he had managed to lend the entire sum to a desperate friend and was now obliged to await its return. A rather mysterious case to say the least of it. Ardalion maintained that it was a "matter of honor." I, on my part, am always most skeptical about such vague matters which involve honor—and, mark you, not the honor of the ragged borrower himself, but always that of a third or even fourth party, whose name is not disclosed. Ardalion (always according to his tale) *had* to lend the money, the other swearing he would return it within three days; the usual time limit with those descendants of feudal barons. When that time had expired Ardalion went to look for his debtor and, naturally, could not find him anywhere. With icy fury, I asked for his name. Ardalion attempted to evade the question and then said: "Oh, you remember—that fellow who once called on you." That made me lose my temper altogether.

Upon regaining my calm, I would have probably helped him out, had not things been complicated by my being rather short of money, whereas it was absolutely necessary that I should have a certain amount about me. I told him to set forth as he was, with a ticket and a few marks in his pocket. I'd send him the rest, I said. He answered that he would do so, just postponing his departure for a couple of days in case the money might still be retrieved. And indeed on the third of March he rang me up to say, rather casually, I thought, that he had got back his loan and was starting next evening. On the fourth it turned out that Lydia, to whom, for some reason or other, Ardalion had given his ticket to keep for him, was at present incapable of recalling where she had put it. A gloomy Ardalion crouched on a stool in the hall: "Nothing to be done," he muttered repeatedly. "Fate is against it." From the adjoining rooms there came the banging of drawers and a frantic rustling of paper: it was Lydia hunting for the ticket. An hour later Ardalion gave up and went home. Lydia sat on the bed crying her heart out. On the fifth she discovered the ticket among the dirty linen prepared for the laundry; and on the sixth we went to see Ardalion off.

The train was due to leave at 10:10. The longer hand of the clock would point like a setter, then pounce on the coveted minute, and forthwith aim at the next. No Ardalion. We stood waiting beside the coach marked "Milan."

"What on earth is the matter," Lydia kept worrying. "Why doesn't he come? I'm anxious."

All that ridiculous fuss about Ardalion's departure maddened me to such an extent that I was now afraid to unclench my teeth lest I have a fit or something on the station platform. Two sordid individuals, one sporting a blue mackintosh, the other a Russian-looking greatcoat with a moth-eaten astrakhan collar, came up and, dodging me, effusively greeted Lydia.

"Why doesn't he come? What d'you think has happened?" Lydia asked, looking at them with frightened eyes and holding away from her the little bunch of violets which she had taken the trouble to buy for the brute. The blue mackintosh spread out his hands, and the fur collar pronounced in a deep voice:

"*Nescimus*. We do not know."

I felt I could not contain myself any longer and, turning sharply, marched off toward the exit. Lydia ran after me: "Where are you going, wait a bit, I'm sure he's—"

It was at this minute that Ardalion appeared in the distance. A grim-faced tatterdemalion held him up by the elbow and carried his portmanteau. So drunk was Ardalion that he could barely stand on his feet; the grim one, too, reeked of spirits.

"Oh, dear, he can't go in such a state," cried Lydia.

Very flushed, very humid, bewildered and groggy, without his overcoat (in hazy anticipation of southern warmth), Ardalion started upon a tottering round of slobbery embraces. I just managed to avoid him.

"My name's Perebrodov, professional artist," blurted his grim companion, confidentially thrusting out, as if it held a dirty postcard, an unshakable hand in my direction. "Had the fortune of meeting you in the gambling hells of Cairo."

"Hermann, do something! Impossible to let him go like that," wailed Lydia tugging at my sleeve.

Meanwhile the carriage doors were already slamming. Ardalion, swaying and emitting appealing cries, had reeled off to follow the cart of a sandwich-and-brandy vendor, but was caught by friendly hands. Then, all at once, he gathered up Lydia in his clutch and covered her with juicy kisses.

"Oh, you googly kid," he cooed, "good-bye, kid, thanks, kid. . . ."

"Look here, gentlemen," said I with perfect calm, "would you mind helping me to lift him into the carriage?"

The train glided off. Beaming and bawling, Ardalion all

but tumbled out of the window. Lydia, a lamb in leopard's clothes, trotted alongside the carriage almost as far as Switzerland. When the last carriage turned its buffers upon her, she bent low, peering under the receding wheels (a national superstition) and then crossed herself. She still held in her fist that little bunch of violets.

Ah, what relief. . . . The sigh I heaved filled my chest and I let it out noisily. All day long Lydia gently fretted and worried, but then a wire came—two words: "Traveling merrily"—and that soothed her. I had now to tackle the most tedious part of the business: talking to her, coaching her.

I fail to remember the way I began: when the current of my memory is turned on, that talk is already in full swing. I see Lydia sitting on the divan and staring at me with dumb amazement. I see myself sitting on the edge of a chair opposite her and now and then, like a doctor, touching her wrist. I hear my even voice going on and on. First I told her something, which, I said, I had never told anyone before. I told her about my younger brother. He was a student in Germany when the war broke out; was recruited there and fought against the Russians. I had always remembered him as a quiet, despondent little fellow. My parents used to thrash *me* and spoil *him;* he did not show them any affection, however, but in regard to me he developed an incredible, more than brotherly adoration, followed me everywhere, looked into my eyes, loved everything that came into contact with me, loved to smell my pocket handkerchief, to put on my shirt when still warm from my body, to clean his teeth with my brush. At first we shared a bed with a pillow at each end until it was discovered he could not go to sleep without sucking my big toe, whereupon I was expelled to a mattress in the lumber room but since he insisted on changing places with me in the middle of the night, we never quite knew, nor did dear mamma, who was sleeping where. It was not a perversion on his part—oh, not at all—it was but the best he could do to express our indescribable oneness, for we resembled each other so closely that our nearest relatives used to mistake us, and as the years went on, this resemblance grew more and more perfect. I remember that when I was seeing him off on his way to Germany (that was shortly before Princip's pistol shot) the poor fellow sobbed with such bitterness as though he foresaw what a long and cruel separation it would be. People on the platform looked at us, looked at those two identical youths who stood with interlocked hands and peered into each other's eyes with a kind of sorrowful ecstasy. . . .

Then came the war. Whilst languishing in remote captivity I never had any news of my brother, but was somehow sure that he had been killed. Sultry years, black-shrouded years. I taught myself not to think of him; and even later, when I was married, not a word thereof did I breathe to Lydia—it was all too sad.

Then, soon after my bringing my wife to Germany, a cousin (who took his cue in passing, just to utter that single line) informed me that Felix, though alive, had morally perished. I never learned the exact manner in which his soul was wrecked. . . . Presumably, his delicate psychic structure did not withstand the strain of war, while the thought that I was no more (for, strange to say, he, too, was sure of his brother's death), that never would he see his adored double, or better say, the optimal edition of his own personality, this thought crippled his mind, he felt as if he had lost both support and ambition, so that henceforth life could be lived anyhow. And down he went. That man as sweet-tuned as some musical instrument now turned thief and forger, took to drugs and finally committed murder: he poisoned the woman who kept him. I learned of the latter affair from his own lips; he had not even been suspected—so cunningly had the evil deed been concealed. As to my meeting him again . . . well, that was the work of chance, a most unexpected and painful meeting too (one of its consequences being that change in me, that depression which even Lydia had noticed) in a café at Prague: he stood up, I remember, upon seeing me, opened his arms and crashed backward in a deep swoon which lasted eighteen minutes.

Yes, horribly painful. Instead of the sluggish, dreamy, tender lad, I found a talkative madman, all jerks and jumps. The happiness he experienced upon being reunited with me, dear old Hermann, who all at once, dressed in a handsome grey suit, had arisen from the dead, not only did not lull his conscience, but quite, quite contrariwise, convinced him of the utter inadmissibility of living with a murder on his mind. The conversation we had was awful; he kept covering my hands with kisses, and bidding me farewell. Even the waiters wept.

Very soon I realized that no human force in the world could now shake the decision he had formed of killing himself; even I could do nothing, I who always had had such an ideal influence on him. The minutes I lived through were anything but pleasant. Putting myself in his shoes, I could readily imagine the refined torture which his memory made him endure; and I perceived, alas, that the sole issue for him was death. God forbid anyone passing through such an ordeal —that is, seeing one's brother perish and not having the moral right to avert his doom.

But now comes the complication: his soul, which had its

mystical side, yearned for some atonement, some sacrifice: merely putting a bullet through his brain seemed to him not sufficient.

"I want to make a gift of my death to somebody," he suddenly said and his eyes brimmed with the diamond light of madness. "Make a gift of my death. We two are still more alike than we were formerly. In our sameness I see a divine intent. To lay one's hands upon a piano does not yet mean the making of music, and what I want is music. Tell me, might it not benefit you in some way to vanish from the earth?"

At first, I did not heed his question: I supposed that Felix was delirious; and a gypsy orchestra in the café drowned part of his speech; his subsequent words proved, however, that he had a definite plan. So! On one hand the abyss of a soul in torment, on the other, business prospects. In the lurid glare of his tragic fate and belated heroism, that part of his plan which concerned me, my profit, my well-being, seemed as stupidly matter of fact, as, say, the inauguration of a railway during an earthquake.

Having arrived at this point of my story, I stopped speaking, and, leaning back in my chair with folded arms, looked fixedly at Lydia. She seemed to flow down from the couch on to the carpet, crawled up to me on her knees, pressed her head against my thigh and, in a hushed voice started comforting me: "Oh, you poor, poor thing," she purred. "I'm so sorry for you, for your brother. . . . Heavens, what unhappy people there are in the world! He mustn't die, it is never impossible to save a person."

"He can't be saved," said I, with what is called, I believe, a bitter smile. "He is determined to die on his birthday; the ninth of March—that is to say, the day after tomorrow; and the President of the State could not prevent it. Suicide is the worst form of self-indulgence. All one can do is to comply with the martyr's whim and brighten up things for him by granting him the knowledge that in dying he performs a good useful deed—of a crude material nature, perhaps, but anyhow, useful."

Lydia hugged my leg and stared up at me.

"His plan is as follows," I went on, in a bland voice: "My life, say, is insured for half a million. In a wood, somewhere, my corpse is found. My widow, that is you—"

"Oh, stop saying such horrors," cried Lydia, scrambling up from the carpet. "I've just been reading a story like that. Oh, do please stop—"

"... My widow, that is you, collects the money. Then she retires to a secluded place abroad. After a while, under an assumed name, I join her and maybe even marry her, if she is good. My real name, you see, will have died with my brother. We resemble each other, don't interrupt, like two drops of blood, and he'll be particularly like me when dead."

"Do stop, do stop! I won't believe there's no way of saving him. . . . Oh, Hermann, how wicked! . . . Where is he actually? —here in Berlin?"

"No, in another part of the country. You keep repeating like a fool: save him, save him. . . . You forget that he is a murderer and a mystic. As to me, I haven't the right to refuse him a little thing that may lighten and adorn his death. You must understand that here we find ourselves entering a higher spiritual plane. It would be one thing if I said to you: 'Look here, old girl, my business is going badly, I'm faced with bankruptcy, also I'm sick of everything and yearn for a remote land, where I'll devote myself to contemplation and poultry breeding, so let us use this rare chance!' But I say nothing of the sort, although I *am* on the brink of ruin and for ages *have* been dreaming, as you know, of life in the lap of Nature. What I do say is something very different, namely: however hard, however terrible it may be, one cannot deny one's own brother the fulfillment of his dying request, one cannot prevent him from doing good—if only posthumous good."

Lydia's eyelids fluttered—I had quite bespit her—but despite the spouting of my speech, she nestled against me, holding me tight. We were both now on the divan, and I continued:

"A refusal of that kind would be a sin. I don't want it. I don't want to load my conscience with a sin of that weight. Do you think I didn't object and try to reason with him? Do you think I found it easy to accept his offer? Do you think I have slept all these nights? I may as well tell you, my dear, that since last year I have been suffering horribly—I would not have my best friend suffer so. Much do I care indeed for that insurance money! But how can I refuse, tell me, how can I deprive him of one last joy—hang it all, it's no good talking!"

I pushed her aside, almost knocking her off the divan, and started marching to and fro. I gulped, I sobbed. Specters of red melodrama reeled.

"You are a million times cleverer than me," half whispered Lydia, wringing her hands (yes, reader, *dixi,* wringing her hands), "but it's all so appalling, so unexpected, I thought it only happened in books. . . . Why, it means . . . oh, everything will change—completely. Our whole life! Why . . . F'rinstance, what about Ardalion?"

"To hell, to hell with him! Here we are discussing the very greatest human tragedy and you plump in with—"

"No, I just asked like that. You've sort of dazed me, my

head feels quite funny. I suppose that—not exactly now, but later on—it will be possible to see him and explain matters. . . . Hermann, what d'you think?"

"Drop worrying about trifles. The future will settle all that. Really, really, really" (my voice suddenly changed to a shrill scream), "what an idiot you are!"

She melted into tears and was all at once a yielding creature quivering on my breast: "Please," she faltered, "please, forgive me. Oh, I'm a fool, you are right, do forgive me! This awful thing happening. Only this morning everything seemed so nice, so clear, so everydayish. Oh, my dear, I'm most terribly sorry for you. I'll do anything you want."

"What I want now is coffee—I am dying for some coffee."

"Come to the kitchen," she said, wiping her tears. "I'll do anything. But please, stay with me, I'm frightened."

In the kitchen. Already appeased, though still sniffing a little, she poured the big brown coffee beans into the open bill of the mill, compressed it between her knees, and began turning the handle. It went stiffly at first, with many a creak and crackle, then there was a sudden easement.

"Imagine, Lydia," said I, sitting on the table and dangling my legs, "imagine that all I'm telling you is fiction. Quite seriously, you know, I've been trying to make myself believe that it was purely an invention of mine or some story I had read somewhere; it was the only way not to go mad with horror. So, listen; the two characters are: an enterprising self-destroyer and his insured double. Now, as the insurance company is not obliged to pay in cases of suicide—"

"I've made it very strong," said Lydia. "You'll like it. Yes, dear, I'm listening."

"—the hero of this cheap mystery story demands the following measures: the thing should be staged in such a manner as to make it appear a plain murder. I do not want to enter into technical details, but here it is in a nutshell: the gun is fastened to a tree trunk, a string tied to the trigger, the suicide turns away, pulling that string, and gets the shot bang in the back. That's a rough outline of the business."

"Oh, wait a bit," cried Lydia, "I've remembered something: he somehow fixed the revolver to the bridge ... No, that's wrong: he first tied a stone with a string ... let me see, how did it go? Oh, I've got it: he tied a big stone to one end and the revolver to the other, and then shot himself. And the stone fell in the water, and the string followed across the parapet, and the revolver came next—all splash into the water. Only I can't remember why it was necessary."

"Smooth water, in brief; and a dead man left on the bridge. What a good thing coffee is! I had a splitting headache; now it's much better. So that's clear to you, more or less—I mean the way it all has to happen."

I sipped the fiery coffee and meditated the while. Odd, she had no imagination whatever. In a couple of days life changes —topsy-turvy ... a regular earthquake ... and here she was, comfortably drinking coffee with me and recalling some Sherlock Holmes adventure.

I was mistaken, however: Lydia started and said, slowly lowering her cup:

"I'm just thinking, Hermann, that if it's all going to be so soon, then we ought to begin packing. And, oh, dear, there's all that linen in the wash. And your tuxedo is at the cleaner's."

"First, my dear, I am not particularly anxious to be cremated in evening dress; secondly, pluck out of your head, quick and for good, the idea that you ought to act somehow, to prepare things and so on. There is nothing you ought to do, for the simple reason that you know nothing, nothing whatever—make a mental note of that, if you please. So, no mysterious allusions in front of your friends, no bustle, no shopping—let that sink in, my good woman—otherwise we'll all get into trouble. I repeat: you know nothing as yet. After tomorrow your husband goes for a drive in his car and fails to return. It is then, and only then, that your work begins. Very responsible work, though quite simple. Now I want you to listen with the utmost attention. On the morning of the tenth you'll phone to Orlovius telling him I've gone, not slept at home and not yet returned. You'll ask what to do about it. And act according to his advice. Let him, generally, take full possession of the case, doing everything, such as informing the police, et cetera. The body will turn up very soon. It is essential that you should make yourself believe I'm really dead. As things stand it won't be very far from the truth, as my brother is part of my soul."

"I'd do anything," she said, "anything for his sake and yours. Only I'm dreadfully frightened, and it is all getting mixed up in my head."

"Let it not get mixed up. The chief thing is naturalness of grief. It may not exactly bleach your hair but it must be natural. In order to make your task easier I've given Orlovius a hint to the effect that you've ceased loving me for years. So let it be the quiet reserved sort of sorrow. Sigh and be silent. Then when you see my corpse, that is, the corpse of a man undistinguishable from me, you're sure to get a real good shock."

"Ugh! I can't, Hermann! I'll die of fright."

"It would be worse if right in the mortuary you started

powdering your nose. In any case, contain yourself. Don't scream, or else it'll be necessary after the screams, to raise the general level of your grief, and you know what a bad actress you are. Now let us proceed. The policy and my testament are in the middle drawer of my desk. After having had my body burnt, in agreement with my testament, after settling all formalities, after receiving, through Orlovius, your due, and doing with the money what he tells you to, you'll go abroad to Paris. Where will you stop in Paris?"

"I don't know, Hermann."

"Try and remember where it was we put up when we were in Paris together. Well?"

"Yes, it's coming back to me now. Hotel."

"But what hotel?"

"I can't remember a thing, Hermann, when you keep looking at me like that. I tell you it's coming back. Hotel something."

"I'll give you a tip: it has to do with grass. What is the French for grass?"

"Wait a sec—*herbe*. Oh, got it; Malherbe."

"To be quite safe, in case you forget again, you can always look at your black trunk. There's the hotel label on it still."

"Look here, Hermann, I'm really not such a muff as all that. Though I think I'd better take that trunk. The black one."

"So that's the place you stop at. Next there comes something extremely important. First, however, I'll trouble you to say it all over again."

"I'll be sad. I'll try not to cry too much. Orlovius. Two black dresses and a veil."

"Not so fast. What will you do when you see the body?"

"Fall on my knees. *Not* scream."

"That's right. You see how nicely it all shapes out. Well, what comes next?"

"Next I'll have him buried."

"In the first place not him, but me. Please, don't get that muddled. In the second: not burial, but cremation. Nobody wants to be disinhumed. Orlovius will inform the pastor of my merits; moral, civic, matrimonial. The pastor in the crematorium chapel will deliver a heartfelt speech. To the sound of organ music my coffin will slowly sink into Hades. That's all. What after that?"

"After that—Paris. No, wait! First, all kinds of money formalities. I'm afraid, you know, Orlovius will bore me to death. Then, in Paris, I'll go to the hotel—now I knew it would happen, I just thought I'd forget and so I have. You sort of oppress me. Hotel ... Hotel ... Oh—Malherbe! For safety—the trunk."

"Black. Now comes the important bit: as soon as you get to Paris, you let me know. What method should I adopt to make you memorize the address?"

"Better write it down, Hermann. My brain simply refuses to work at present. I'm so horribly afraid I shall bungle it all."

"No, my dear, I shan't write down anything. If only for the reason that you're bound to lose anything put down in writing. You'll have to memorize the address whether you like it or not. There is absolutely no other way. I forbid you once and for all to write it down. That clear?"

"Yes, Hermann, but what if I *can't* remember?"

"Nonsense. The address is quite simple. Post office, Pignan, France."

"That's where Aunt Elisa used to live? Oh, yes, that's not hard to remember. But she lives near Nice now. Better go to Nice."

"Good idea, but I shan't. Now comes the name. For the sake of simplicity I suggest you write thus: Monsieur Malherbe."

"She is probably as fat and as lively as ever. D'you know, Ardalion wrote to her asking for money, but of course—"

"Most interesting, I'm sure, but we were talking of business. What name will you write on the address?"

"You haven't told me yet, Hermann!"

"Yes, I have. I suggest Monsieur Malherbe."

"But . . . that's the hotel, Hermann, isn't it?"

"Exactly. That's why. You'll find it easier to remember by association."

"Oh, Lord, I'm sure to forget the association, Hermann. I'm hopeless. Please, let's not have any associations. Besides— it's getting awfully late, I'm exhausted."

"Then think of a name yourself. Some name you're practically certain to remember. Would perhaps Ardalion do?"

"Very well, Hermann."

"So that's settled too. Monsieur Ardalion. Post office, Pignan. Now the contents. You'll begin: 'Dear friend, you have surely heard about my bereavement'—and so on in the same gist. A few lines in all. You'll post the letter yourself. You'll post the letter yourself. Got that?"

"Very well, Hermann."

"Now, will you please, repeat."

"You know the strain is too much for me, I'm going to collapse. Good heavens, half-past one. Couldn't we leave it till tomorrow?"

"Tomorrow you will have to repeat it all the same. Come, let's get it over. I'm listening. . . ."

"Hotel Malherbe. I arrive. I post that letter. Myself. Ardalion. Post office, Pignan, France. And after I've written, what next?"

"No concern of yours. We'll see. Well, can I be certain you'll manage it properly?"

"Yes, Hermann. Only don't make me say it all over again. I'm dead beat."

Standing in the middle of the kitchen, she expanded her shoulders, threw back her head and shook it violently, and said several times, her hands worrying her hair: "Oh, how tired I am, oh, how—" that "how" opened into a yawn. We turned in at last. She undressed, scattering about the room frock, stockings, various feminine odds and ends; tumbled into bed and settled down at once to a comfortable nasal wheeze. I went to bed too and put out the light, but could not sleep. I remember she suddenly awoke and touched my shoulder.

"What d'you want?" I inquired feigning drowsiness.

"Hermann," she muttered: "Hermann, tell me, I wonder if ... don't you think it's ... a swindle?"

"Go to sleep," I replied. "Your brains are not equal to the job. Deep tragedy ... and you with your nonsense ... go to sleep!"

She sighed blissfully, turned on her side and was immediately snoring again.

Curious, although I did not deceive myself in the least regarding my wife's capacities, well knowing how stupid, forgetful and clumsy she was, I had, somehow, no misgivings, so absolutely did I believe that her devotion would make her take, instinctively, the right course, preserving her from any slip, and, what mattered most, forcing her to keep my secret. In fancy I clearly saw the way Orlovius would glance at her bad imitation of sorrow and sadly wag his solemn head, and (who knows) ponder perhaps upon the likelihood of the poor husband's having been done in by the lady's paramour; but then that threatening letter from the nameless lunatic would come to him as a timely reminder.

The whole of the next day we spent at home, and once more, meticulously and strenuously, I kept tutoring my wife, stuffing her with my will, just as a goose is crammed, by force, with maize to fatten its liver. By nightfall she was scarcely able to walk; I remained satisfied with her condition. It was time for me to get ready too. I remember how I racked my brains for hours, calculating what sum to take with me, what to leave Lydia; there was not much cash, not much at all . . . it occurred to me that it would be wise to take some valuable thing, so I said to Lydia:

"Look here, give me your Moscow brooch."

"Ah, yes, the brooch," she said dully; slunk out of the room, but immediately came back, lay down on the divan and began to cry as she had never yet cried before.

"What's the matter, you wretched woman?"

For a long while she did not answer, and then, amid much silly sobbing, and with averted eyes, explained that the diamond brooch, an empress's gift to her great-grandmother, had been pawned to obtain the money for Ardalion's journey, as his friend had not repaid him.

"All right, all right, don't howl," I said, pocketing the pawn ticket. "Deuced cunning of him. Thank God he's gone, scuttled away—that's the main thing."

She instantly regained her composure and even achieved a dew-bright smile when she saw I was not cross. Then she tripped off to the bedroom, was long rummaging there, and finally brought me a cheap little ring, a pair of eardrops, an old-fashioned cigarette-case that had belonged to her mother. . . . None of these things did I take.

"Listen," said I, wandering about the room and biting my thumb. "Listen, Lydia. When they ask you if I had enemies, when they examine you as to who might have killed me, reply: 'I don't know.' And there's something else: I'm taking a suitcase with me, but that's strictly confidential. It ought not to appear as though I was getting ready for a journey—that would be suspicious. As a matter of fact—"

At that point I remember stopping suddenly. How queer it was that when all had been so beautifully devised and foreseen, there should come sticking out a minor detail, as when you are packing and notice all at once that you have forgotten to put in some small but cumbersome trifle—yes, there do exist such unscrupulous objects. It should be said, to my justification, that the question of the suitcase was really the only point which I decided to alter: all the rest went just as I had designed it long, long ago—maybe many months ago, maybe that very second when I saw a tramp asleep on the grass who exactly resembled my corpse. No, thought I, better not take the suitcase; there is always the risk of somebody seeing me leaving the house with it.

"I'm not taking it," said I aloud, and went on pacing the room.

How can I forget the morning of the ninth of March? As mornings go, it was pale and cold; overnight some snow had fallen, and now every house porter was sweeping his stretch of sidewalk along which there ran a low snow ridge, whereas the asphalt was already clean and black—only a little slimy. Lydia slept on in peace. All was quiet. I began the business of dressing. That is how it went: two shirts, one over the other; yesterday's one on top, as it was meant for him. Drawers —also two pairs; and again the top pair was for him. Then

I made a small parcel containing a manicure set, a shaving kit, and a shoehorn. So as not to forget, I at once slipped that parcel into the pocket of my overcoat which hung in the hall. Then I put on two pairs of socks (the top one with a hole in it), black shoes, mouse-grey spats; and, arrayed thus, i.e., smartly shod but still in my undergarments, I stood in the middle of the room and mentally checked my actions so as to see whether they conformed to plan. Remembering that an extra pair of garters would be required I unearthed some old ones and added them to the parcel, which necessitated my coming out again into the hall. Lastly, I chose my favorite lilac tie and a thick dark-grey suit I had been often wearing lately. The following objects were distributed among pockets: my wallet (with something like fifteen hundred marks in it), passport, sundry scraps of paper with addresses, accounts.

Stop, that's wrong, I said to myself, for had I not decided *not* to take my passport? A very subtle move, that: the casual scraps of paper established one's identity more gracefully. I also took keys, cigarette-case, lighter. Strapped on my wrist-watch. Now I was dressed. I patted my pockets, I puffed slightly. I felt rather warm in my double cocoon. There now remained the most important item. Quite a ceremony; the slow glide of the drawer where IT rested, a careful examination, and not the first one, to be sure. Yes, IT was admirably oiled; IT was chock full of good things.... IT was given to me in 1920, in Reval, by an unknown officer; or, to be precise, he simply left IT with me and vanished. I have no idea what became of that amiable lieutenant afterwards.

While I was thus engaged, Lydia awoke. She wrapped herself up in a dressing gown of a sickly pink hue and we sat down to our morning coffee. When the maid had left the room:

[ 152 ]

"Well," I said, "the day has come! I'm going in a minute."

A very slight digression of a literary nature; that rhythm is foreign to modern speech, but it renders, especially well, my epic calm and the dramatic tension of the situation.

"Hermann, please stay, don't go anywhere. . . ." said Lydia in a low voice (and she even joined her hands together, I believe).

"You remember everything, don't you?" I went on imperturbably.

"Hermann," she repeated, "don't go. Let him do whatever he likes, it's his fate, you mustn't interfere."

"I'm glad you remember everything," said I with a smile. "Good girl. Now let me eat one more roll and I'll start."

She broke into tears. Then blew her nose with a last blast, was about to say something, but began crying anew. It was rather a quaint scene; I, coolly buttering a horn-shaped roll, she, seated opposite, her whole frame shaken by sobs. I said, with my mouth full:

"Anyway, you'll be able, in front of the world" (I chewed and swallowed here), "to recall that you had evil forebodings, although I used to go away fairly often and never said where. 'And do you know, madam, if he had any enemies?' 'I don't, Mr. Coroner.' "

"But what's going to come next?" Lydia gently moaned, slowly and helplessly moving her hands apart.

"That'll do, my dear," said I, in another tone of voice. "You've had your little cry and now it's enough. And, by the way, don't dream of howling today in Elsie's presence."

She dabbed at her eyes with a crumpled handkerchief, emitted a sad little grunt and once again made that gesture of helpless perplexity, but now in silence and without tears.

"You remember everything?" I inquired for the last time, narrowly scrutinizing her.

"Yes, Hermann, everything. But I'm so, so frightened. . . ."

I stood up, she stood up too. I said:

"Good-bye. See you some day. Time to go to my patient."

"Hermann, tell me—you don't intend being present, do you?"

I quite failed to see what she meant.

"Present? At what?"

"Oh, you know what I'm thinking. When he—oh, you know . . . that business of the string."

"You goose," said I, "what did you expect? Somebody must be there to tidy up afterwards. Now I'll trouble you not to brood any more over the matter. Go to the pictures tonight. Good-bye, goose."

I never kissed her on the mouth: I loathe the slush of lip kisses. It is said, the ancient Slavs, too—even in moments of sexual excitement never kissed their women—found it queerish, perhaps even a little repulsive, to bring into contact one's own naked lips with another's epithelium. At that moment, however, I felt, for once, an impulse to kiss my wife that way; but she was unprepared, so, somehow, nothing came of it, except that I grazed her hair with my lips; I refrained from making another attempt, instead of which I clicked my heels and shook her listless hand. Then, in the hall, I rapidly got into my overcoat, snatched my gloves, ascertained whether I had the parcel, and when already making for the door, heard her call me from the dining room in a low whimpering voice, but I did not take much notice as I was in a desperate hurry to leave.

I crossed the back yard towards a large garage packed with

cars. Pleasant smiles welcomed me there. I got in and started the engine. The asphalted surface of the yard was somewhat higher than that of the street so that upon entering the narrow inclined tunnel connecting the yard with the street, my car, held back by its brakes, lightly and noiselessly dipped.

# Chapter Nine

To tell the truth, I feel rather weary. I keep on writing from noon to dawn, producing a chapter per day—or more. What a great powerful thing art is! In my situation, I ought to be flustering, scurrying, doubling back.... There is of course no immediate danger, and I dare say such danger there will never be, but, nevertheless, it is a singular reaction, this sitting still and writing, writing, writing, or ruminating at length, which is much the same, really. And the further I write, the clearer it becomes that I will not leave matters so but hang on till my main object is attained, when I will most certainly take the risk of having my work published—not much of a risk, either, for as soon as my manuscript is sent out I shall fade away, the world being large enough to afford a place of concealment to a quiet man with a beard.

It was not spontaneously that I decided to forward my work to the penetrating novelist, whom, I think, I have mentioned already, even addressing him personally through the medium of my story.

I may be mistaken, as I have long ago abandoned reading over what I write—no time left for that, let alone its nauseating effect upon me.

I had first toyed with the idea of sending the thing straight to some editor—German, French, or American—but it is written in Russian and not all is translatable, and—well, to be frank, I am rather particular about my literary coloratura and firmly believe that the loss of a single shade or inflection would hopelessly mar the whole. I have also thought of sending it to the U.S.S.R., but I lack the necessary addresses, nor do I know how it is done and whether my manuscript would be read, for I employ, by force of habit, the Old-Regime spelling, and to rewrite it would be quite beyond my powers. Did I say "rewrite"? Well, I hardly know if I shall stand the strain of writing it at all.

Having at last made up my mind to give my manuscript to one who is sure to like it and do his best to have it published, I am fully aware of the fact that my chosen one (you, my first reader) is an *émigré* novelist, whose books cannot possibly appear in the U.S.S.R. Maybe, however, an exception will be made for this book, considering that it was not you who actually wrote it. Oh, how I cherish the hope that in spite of your *émigré* signature (the diaphanous spuriousness of which will deceive nobody) my book may find a market in the U.S.S.R.! As I am far from being an enemy of the Soviet rule, I am sure to have unwittingly expressed certain notions in my book, which correspond perfectly to the dialectical demands of the current moment. It even seems to me sometimes that my basic theme, the resemblance between two persons, has a profound allegorical meaning. This remarkable physical likeness probably appealed to me (subconsciously!) as the promise of that ideal sameness which is to unite people in the classless society of the future; and by striving to make use of an isolated case, I was, though still blind to social truths, fulfilling, nevertheless, a certain social function. And then there is something else; the fact of my not being wholly successful when putting that resemblance of ours to practical use can be explained away by purely social-economic causes, that is to say, by the fact that Felix and I belonged to different, sharply defined classes, the fusion of which none can hope to achieve single-handed, especially nowadays, when the conflict of classes has reached a stage where compromise is out of the question. True, my mother was of low birth and my father's father herded geese in his youth, which explains where, exactly, a man of my stamp and habits could have got that strong, though still incompletely expressed leaning towards Genuine Consciousness. In fancy, I visualize a new world, where all men will resemble one another as Hermann and Felix did; a world of Helixes and Fermanns; a world where the worker fallen dead at the feet of his machine will be at once replaced by his perfect double smiling the serene smile of perfect socialism. Therefore I do think that Soviet youths of today should derive considerable benefit from a study of my book under the supervision of an experienced Marxist who would help them to follow through its pages the rudimentary wriggles of the social message it contains. Aye, let other nations, too, translate it into their respective languages, so that American readers may satisfy their craving for gory glamour; the French discern mirages of sodomy in my partiality for a vagabond; and Germans relish the skittish side of a semi-Slavonic soul. Read, read it, as many as possible, ladies and gentlemen! I welcome you all as my readers.

Not an easy book to write, though. It is now especially, just as I am getting to the part which treats, so to speak, of decisive action, it is now that the arduousness of my task appears to me in full; here I am, as you see, twisting and turning and being garrulous about matters which rightly belong to the preface of a book and are misplaced in what the reader may deem its most essential chapter. But I have tried to explain already that, however shrewd and wary the approaches may seem, it is not my rational part which is writing, but solely my memory, that devious memory of mine. For, you see, *then,* i.e. at the precise hour at which the hands of my story have stopped, I had stopped too; was dallying, as I am dallying now; was engaged in a similar kind of tangled reasoning having nothing to do with my business, the appointed hour of which was steadily nearing. I had started in the morning though my meeting with Felix was fixed for five o'clock in the afternoon, but I had been unable to stay at home, so that now I was wondering how to dispose of all that dull-white mass of time separating me from my appointment. I sat at my ease, even somnolently, as I steered with one finger and slowly drove through Berlin, down quiet, cold, whispering streets; and so it went on and on, until I noticed that I had left Berlin behind. The colors of the day were reduced to a mere two: black (the pattern of the bare trees, the asphalt) and whitish (the sky, the patches of snow). It continued, my sleepy transportation. For some time there dangled before my eyes one of those large, ugly rags that a truck trundling something long and poky is required to hang on the protruding hind end; then it disappeared, having presumably taken a turning. Still I did not move on any quicker. A taxicab dashed out of a side street in front of me, put on the brakes with a screech, and owing to the road being rather slippery, went into a grotesque spin. I calmly sailed past, as if drifting downstream. Farther, a woman in deep mourning was crossing obliquely, practically with her back to me; I neither sounded my horn, nor changed my quiet smooth motion, but glided past within a couple of inches from the edge of her veil; she did not even notice me—a noiseless ghost. Every kind of vehicle overtook me; for quite a while a crawling tramcar kept abreast of me; and out of the corner of my eye I could see the passengers, stupidly sitting face to face. Once or twice I struck a badly cobbled stretch; and hens were already appearing; short wings expanded and long necks stretched out, this fowl or that would come running across the road. A little later I found myself driving along an endless highway, past stubbled fields with snow lying here and there; and in a perfectly deserted locality my car seemed to sink into a slumber, as if turning from blue to dove-grey—slowing down gradually and coming to a stop, and I leaned my head on the wheel in a fit of elusive musing. What could my thoughts be about? About nothing or nothings; it was all very involved and I was almost asleep, and in a half swoon I kept deliberating with myself about some nonsense, kept remembering some discussion I had had with somebody once on some station platform as to whether one ever sees the sun in one's dreams, and presently the feeling grew upon me that there was a great number of people around, all speaking together, and then falling silent and giving one another dim errands and dispersing without a sound. After some time I moved on, and at noon, dragging through some village, I decided to halt, since even at such a drowsy pace I was bound to reach Koenigsdorf in an hour or so, and that was still too early. So I dawdled in a dark and dismal beer house, where I sat quite alone in a back room of sorts, at a big table, and there was an old photograph on the wall—a group of men in frock coats, with curled-up moustachios, and some in the front row had bent one knee with a carefree expression and two at the sides had even stretched themselves seal fashion, and this called to my mind similar groups of Russian students. I had a lot of lemon water there and resumed my journey in the same sleepy mood, quite indecently sleepy, in fact. Next, I remember stopping at some bridge: an old woman in blue woolen trousers and with a bag behind her shoulders was busy repairing some mishap to her bicycle. Without getting out of my car I gave her several pieces of advice, all quite unbidden and useless; and after that I was silent, and propping my cheek with my fist, remained gaping at her for a long time: there she was fussing and fussing, but at last my eyelids twitched and lo, there was no woman there: she had wobbled away long ago. I pursued my course, trying, as I did, to multiply in my head one uncouth number by another just as awkward. I did not know what they signified and whence they had floated up, but since they had come I considered it fit to bait them, and so they grappled and dissolved. All of a sudden it struck me that I was driving at a crazy speed; that the car was lapping up the road, like a conjurer swallowing yards of ribbon; but I glanced at the speedometer-needle: it was trembling at fifty kilometers; and there passed by, in slow succession, pines, pines, pines. Then, too, I remember meeting two small pale-faced schoolboys with their books held together by a strap; and I talked to them. They both had unpleasant birdlike features, making me think of young crows. They seemed to be a little afraid of me, and when I drove off, kept staring after me, black mouths wide open, one taller, the other shorter. And then, with a start, I noticed that I had reached Koenigsdorf and, looking at my watch, saw that it was almost five. When passing the red station-building, I reflected that perchance Felix was late and had not yet come down those steps I saw beyond that gaudy chocolate-stand, and that there were no means whatever of deducing from the exterior air of that squat brick edifice whether he had already passed there or not. However that might be, the train by which he had been ordered to come to Koenigsdorf arrived at 2:55, so that if Felix had not missed it—

Oh, my reader! He had been told to get off at Koenigsdorf and march north following the highway as far as the tenth kilometer marked by a yellow post; and now I was tearing along that road: unforgettable moments! Not a soul about. During winter the bus ran there but twice a day—morning and noon; on the entire ten kilometers' stretch all that I met was a cart drawn by a bay horse. At last, in the distance, like a yellow finger, the familiar post stood up, grew bigger, attained its natural size; it wore a skullcap of snow. I pulled up and looked about me. Nobody. The yellow post was very yellow indeed. To my right, beyond the field, the wood was painted a flat grey on the backdrop of the pale sky. Nobody. I got out of my car and with a bang that was louder than any shot, slammed the door after me. And all at once I noticed that, from behind the interlaced twigs of a bush growing in the ditch, there stood looking at me, as pink as a waxwork and with a jaunty little mustache, and, really, quite gay—

Placing one foot on the footboard of the car and like an enraged tenor slashing my hand with the glove I had taken off, I glared steadily at Felix. Grinning uncertainly, he came out of the ditch.

"You scoundrel," I uttered through my teeth with extraordinary operatic force, "you scoundrel and double-crosser," I repeated, now giving my voice full scope and slashing myself with the glove still more furiously (all was rumble and thunder in the orchestra between my vocal outbursts). "How did you dare blab, you cur? How did you dare, how did you dare ask others for advice, boast that you had had your way and that at such a date and at such a place— Oh, you deserve to be shot!"—(growing din, clangor, and then again my voice)— "Much have you gained, idiot! The game's up, you've blundered badly, not a groat will you see, baboon!" (crash of cymbals in the orchestra).

Thus I swore at him, with cold avidity observing the while his expression. He was utterly taken aback; and honestly offended. Pressing one hand to his breast, he kept shaking his head. That fragment of opera came to an end, and the broadcast speaker resumed in his usual voice:

"Let it pass—I've been scolding you like that, as a pure formality, to be on the safe side. . . . My dear fellow, you do look funny, it's a regular makeup!"

By my special order, he had let his mustache grow; even waxed it, I think. Apart from that, on his own account, he had allowed his face a couple of curled cutlets. I found that pretentious growth highly entertaining.

"You have, of course, come by the way I told you?" I inquired, smiling.

"Yes," he replied, "I followed your orders. As for bragging —well, you know yourself, I'm a lonely man and no good at chatting with people."

"I know, and join you in your sighs. Tell me, did you meet anyone on this road?"

"When I saw a cart or something, I hid in the ditch, as you told me to do."

"Splendid. Your features anyhow are sufficiently concealed. Well, no good loafing about here. Get into the car. Oh, leave that alone—you'll take off your bag afterwards. Get in quick, we must drive off."

"Where to?" he queried.

"Into that wood."

"There?" he asked and pointed with his stick.

"Yes, right there. Will you or won't you get in, damn you?"

He surveyed the car contentedly. Without hurry he climbed in and sat down beside me.

I turned the steering wheel, with the car slowly moving. Ick. And once again: ick. (We left the road for the field.) Under the tires thin snow and dead grass crackled. The car bounced on humps of ground, we bounced too. He spoke the while:

"I'll manage this car without any trouble (bump). Lord, what a ride I'll take (bump). Never fear (bump-bump) I won't do it any harm!"

"Yes, the car will be yours. For a short space of time (bump) yours. Now, keep awake, my fellow, look about you. There's nobody on the road, is there?"

He glanced back and then shook his head. We drove, or better say crept, up a gentle and fairly smooth slope into the forest. There, among the foremost pines, we stopped and got out. No more with the longing of ogling indigence, but with an owner's quiet satisfaction, Felix continued to admire the glossy blue Icarus. A dreamy look then came into his eyes. Quite likely (please, note that I am asserting nothing, merely saying: "quite likely") quite likely then, his thoughts flowed as follows: "What if I slip away in this natty two-seater? I get the cash in advance, so that's all right. I'll let him believe I'm going to do what he wants, and roll away instead, far away. He just can't inform the police, so he'll have to keep quiet. And me, in my own car—"

I interrupted the course of those pleasant thoughts.

"Well, Felix, the great moment has come. You're to change your clothes and remain in the car all alone in this wood. In half an hour's time it will begin to grow dark; no risk of

anyone intruding upon you. You'll spend the night here—
you'll have my overcoat on—just feel how nice and thick it is
—ah, I thought so; besides, the car is quite warm inside,
you'll sleep perfectly; then, as soon as day begins to break—
But we'll discuss that afterwards; let me first give you the
necessary appearance, or we'll never have done before dark.
To start with, you must have a shave."

"A shave?" Felix repeated after me, with silly surprise.
"How's that? I've got no razor with me, and I really don't
know what one can find in a wood to shave with, barring
stones."

"Why stones? Such a blockhead as you ought to be shaven
with an axe. But I have thought of everything. I've brought
the instrument, and I'll do it myself."

"Well, that's mighty funny," he chuckled. "Wonder what'll
come of it. Now, mind you don't cut my throat with that
razor of yours."

"Don't be afraid, you fool, it's a safety one. So, please. . . .
Yes, sit down somewhere. Here, on the footboard, if you
like."

He sat down after having shaken off his knapsack. I produced my parcel and placed the shaving articles on the footboard. Had to hurry: the day looked pinched and wan, the
air grew duller and duller. And what a hush. . . . It seemed,
that silence, inherent, inseparable from those motionless
boughs, those straight trunks, those lusterless patches of
snow here and there on the ground.

I took off my overcoat so as to operate with more freedom.
Felix was curiously examining the bright teeth of the safety
razor and its silvery grip. Then he examined the shaving
brush; put it to his cheek to test its softness; it was, indeed,
delightfully fluffy: I had paid seventeen marks fifty for it.

He was quite fascinated, too, by the tube of expensive shaving cream.

"Come, let's begin," I said. "Shaving and waving. Sit a little sideways, please, otherwise I can't get at you properly."

I took a handful of snow, squeezed out a curling worm of soap into it, beat it up with the brush and applied the icy lather to his whiskers and mustache. He made faces, leered; a frill of lather had invaded one nostril: he wrinkled his nose, because it tickled.

"Head back," I said, "farther still."

Rather awkwardly resting my knee on the footboard, I started scraping his whiskers off; the hairs crackled, and there was something disgusting in the way they got mixed up with the foam; I cut him slightly, and that stained it with blood. When I attacked his mustache, he puckered up his eyes, but bravely made no sound, although it must have been anything but pleasant: I was working hastily, his bristles were tough, the razor pulled.

"Got a handkerchief?" I asked.

He drew some rag out of his pocket. I used it to wipe away from his face, very carefully, blood, snow and lather. His cheeks shone now—brand new. He was gloriously shaven; in one place only, near the ear, there showed a red scratch running into a little ruby which was about to turn black. He passed his palm over the shaven parts.

"Wait a bit," I said, "that's not all. Your eyebrows need improving: they're somewhat thicker than mine."

I produced scissors and neatly clipped off a few hairs.

"That's capital now. As to your hair, I'll brush it when you've changed your shirt."

"Going to give me yours?" he asked, and deliberately felt the silk of my shirt collar.

"Hullo, your fingernails are not exactly clean!" I exclaimed blithely.

Many a time had I done Lydia's hands—I was good at it, so that now I had not much difficulty in putting those ten rude nails in order, and while doing so I kept comparing our hands: his were larger and darker; but never mind, I thought, they'll pale by and by. As I never wore any wedding ring, all I had to add to his hand was my wristwatch. He moved his fingers, turning his wrist this way and that, very pleased.

"Now, quick. Let's change. Take off everything, my friend, to the last stitch."

"Ugh," grunted Felix, "it'll be cold."

"Never mind. Takes one minute only. Please hurry up."

He removed his old brown coat, pulled off his dark, shaggy sweater over his head. The shirt underneath was a muddy green with a tie of the same material. Then he took off his formless shoes, peeled off his socks (darned by a masculine hand) and hiccuped ecstatically as his bare toe touched the wintry soil. Your common man loves to go barefoot: in summer, on gay grass, the very first thing he does is take off his shoes and socks; but in winter, too, it is no mean pleasure—recalling as it does one's childhood, perhaps, or something like that.

I stood aloof, undoing my cravat, and kept looking at Felix attentively.

"Go on, go on," I cried, noticing that he had slowed down a bit.

It was not without a bashful little squirm that he let his trousers slip down from his white hairless thighs. Lastly he took off his shirt. In the cold wood there stood in front of me a naked man.

Incredibly fast, with the flick and dash of a Fregoli, I undressed, tossed over to him my outer envelope of shirt and drawers, deftly, while he was laboriously putting that on, plucked out of the suit I had shed several things—money, cigarette-case, brooch, gun—and stuffed them into the pockets of the tightish trousers which I had drawn on with the swiftness of a variety virtuoso. Although his sweater proved to be warm enough, I kept my muffler, and as I had lost weight lately, his coat fitted me almost to perfection. Should I offer him a cigarette? No, that would be in bad taste.

Felix meanwhile had attired himself in my shirt and drawers; his feet were still bare, I gave him socks and garters, but noticed all at once that his toes needed some trimming too. . . . He placed his foot on the footboard of the car and we got in a bit of hasty pedicuring. They snapped loud and flew far, those ugly black parings, and in recent dreams I have often seen them speckling the ground much too conspicuously. I am afraid he had time to catch a chill, poor soul, standing there in his shirt. Then he washed his feet with snow, as some bathless rake in Maupassant does, and pulled on the socks, without noticing the hole in one heel.

"Hurry up, hurry up," I kept repeating. "It'll be dark presently, and I must be going. See. I'm already dressed. God, what big shoes! And where is that cap of yours? Ah, here it is, thanks."

He belted the trousers. With the provident help of the shoehorn he squeezed his feet into my black buckskin shoes. I helped him to cope with the spats and the lilac necktie. Finally, gingerly taking his comb, I smoothed his greasy hair well back from brow and temples.

He was ready now. There he stood before me, my double,

in my quiet dark-grey suit. Surveyed himself with a foolish smile. Investigated pockets. Was pleased with the lighter. Replaced the odds and ends, but opened the wallet. It was empty.

"You promised me money in advance," said Felix coaxingly.

"That's right," I replied withdrawing my hand from my pocket and disclosing a fistful of notes. "Here it is. I'll count out your share and give it you in a minute. What about those shoes, do they hurt?"

"They do," said Felix. "They hurt dreadfully. But I'll hold out somehow. I'll take them off for the night, I expect. And where must I go with that car tomorrow?"

"Presently, presently.... I'll make it all clear. Look, the place ought to be tidied up.... You've scattered your rags. ... What have you got in that bag?"

"I'm like a snail, I carry my house on my back," said Felix. "Are you taking the bag with you? I've got half a sausage in it. Like to have some?"

"Later. Pack in all those things, will you? That shoehorn too. And the scissors. Good. Now put on my overcoat and let us verify for the last time whether you can pass for me."

"You won't forget the money?" he inquired.

"I keep on telling you I won't. Don't be an ass. We are on the point of settling it. The cash is here, in my pocket—in your former pocket, to be correct. Now, buck up, please."

He got into my handsome camel-hair overcoat and (with special care) put on my elegant hat. Then came the last touch: yellow gloves.

"Good. Just take a few steps. Let's see how it all fits you."

He came toward me, now thrusting his hands into his pockets, now drawing them out again.

When he got quite near, he squared his shoulders, pretending to swagger, aping a fop.

"Is that all, is that all," I kept saying aloud. "Wait, let me have a thorough— Yes, seems to be all. . . . Now turn, I'd like a back view—"

He turned, and I shot him between the shoulders.

I remember various things: that puff of smoke, hanging in midair, then displaying a transparent fold and vanishing slowly; the way Felix fell; for he did not fall at once; first he terminated a movement still related to life, and that was a full turn almost; he intended, I think, swinging before me in jest, as before a mirror; so that, inertly bringing that poor piece of foolery to an end, he (already pierced) came to face me, slowly spread his hands as if asking: "What's the meaning of this?"—and getting no reply, slowly collapsed backward. Yes, I remember all that; I remember, too, the shuffling sound he made on the snow, when he began to stiffen and jerk, as if his new clothes were uncomfortable; soon he was still, and then the rotation of the earth made itself felt, and only his hat moved quietly, separating from his crown and falling back, mouth opened, as if it were saying "good-bye" for its owner (or again, bringing to one's mind the stale sentence: "all present bared their heads"). Yes, I remember all that, but there is one thing memory misses: the report of my shot. True, there remained in my ears a persistent singing. It clung to me and crept over me, and trembled upon my lips. Through that veil of sound, I went up to the body and, with avidity, looked.

There are mysterious moments and that was one of them. Like an author reading his work over a thousand times, probing and testing every syllable, and finally unable to say of this brindle of words whether it is good or not, so it happened with me, so it happened— But there is the maker's secret certainty; which never can err. At that moment when all the required features were fixed and frozen, our likeness was such that really I could not say who had been killed, I or he. And while I looked, it grew dark in the vibrating wood, and with that face before me slowly dissolving, vibrating fainter and fainter, it seemed as if I were looking at my image in a stagnant pool.

Being afraid to besmirch myself I did not handle the body; did not ascertain whether it was indeed quite, quite dead; I knew instinctively that it was so, that my bullet had slid with perfect exactitude along the short, air-dividing furrow which both will and eye had grooved. Must hurry, must hurry, cried old Mister Murry, as he thrust his arms through his pants. Let us not imitate him. Swiftly, sharply, I looked about me. Felix had put everything, except the pistol, into the bag himself; yet I had self-possession enough to make sure he had not dropped anything; and I even went so far as to brush the footboard where I had been cutting his nails and to unbury his comb which I had trampled into the ground but now decided to discard later. Next I accomplished something planned a long time ago: I had turned the car and stopped it on a bit of timbered ground slightly sloping down, roadward; I now rolled my little Icarus a few yards forward so as to make it visible in the morning from the highway, thus leading to the discovery of my corpse.

Night came sweeping down rapidly. The drumming in my ears had all but died away. I plunged into the wood, repassing as I did so, not far from the body; but I did not stop any more—only picked up the bag, and, unflinchingly, at a smart pace, as if indeed I had not those stone-heavy shoes on my feet, I went round the lake, never leaving the forest, on and on, in the ghostly gloaming, among ghostly snow.... But how beautifully I knew the right direction, how accurately, how vividly I had visualized it all, when, in summer, I used to study the paths leading to Eichenberg!

I reached the station in time. Ten minutes later, with the serviceableness of an apparition, there arrived the train I wanted. I spent half the night in a clattering, swaying third-class carriage, on a hard bench, and next to me were two elderly men, playing cards, and the cards they used were extraordinary: large, red and green, with acorns and beehives. After midnight I had to change; a couple of hours later I was already moving westwards; then, in the morning, I changed anew, this time into a fast train. Only then, in the solitude of the lavatory, did I examine the contents of the knapsack. Besides the things crammed into it lately (blood-stained handkerchief included), I found a few shirts, a piece of sausage, two large apples, a leathern sole, five marks in a lady's purse, a passport; and my letters to Felix. The apples and sausage I ate there and then, in the W.C.; but I put the letters into my pocket and examined the passport with the liveliest interest. It was in good order. He had been to Mons and Metz. Oddly enough, his pictured face did not resemble mine closely; it could, of course, easily pass for my photo—still, that made an odd impression upon me, and I remember thinking that here was the real cause of his being so little aware of our likeness: he saw himself in a glass, that is to say, from right to left, not sunway as in reality. Human fat-headedness, carelessness, slackness of senses, all this was revealed by the fact that even the official definitions in the brief list of personal features did not quite correspond with the epithets in my own passport (left at home). A trifle to be sure, but a characteristic one. And under "profession," he, that numbskull, who had played the fiddle, surely, in the way lackadaisical footmen in Russia used to twang guitars on summer evenings, was called a "musician," which at once turned me into a musician too. Later in the day, at a small border town, I purchased a suitcase, an overcoat, and so forth, upon which both bag and gun were discarded—no, I will not say what I did with them: be silent, Rhenish waters! And presently, a very unshaven gentleman in a cheap black overcoat was on the safer side of the frontier and heading south.

# Chapter Ten

Since childhood I've loved violets and music. I was born at Zwickau. My father was a shoemaker and my mother a washerwoman. When she used to get angry she hissed at me in Czech. Mine was a clouded and joyless childhood. Hardly was I a man than I set forth on my wanderings. I played the fiddle. I'm a left-hander. Face—oval. Not married; show me one wife who is true. I found the war pretty beastly; it passed, however, as all things pass. Every mouse has its house. . . . I like squirrels and sparrows. Czech beer is cheaper. Ah, if one could only get shod by a smith—how economical! All state ministers are bribed, and all poetry is bilge. One day at a fair I saw twins; you were promised a prize if you distinguished between them, so carroty Fritz cuffed one of the two and gave him a thick ear—that was the difference! Golly, what a laugh we had! Beatings, stealings, slaughter, all is bad or good, according to circumstances.

I've appropriated money, whenever it came my way; what you've taken is yours, there is no such thing as one's own or another's money; you don't find written on a coin: belongs to Müller. I like money. I've always wished to find a faithful friend; we'd have made music together, he'd have bequeathed me his house and his orchard. Money, darling money. Darling small money. Darling big money. I roved about; found work here and there. One day I met a swell fellow who kept saying he was like me. Nonsense, he was not like me in the least. But I did not argue with him, he being rich, and whoever hobnobs with the rich can well become rich himself. He wanted me to go for a drive in his stead, leaving him to his business in queer street. I killed the bluffer and robbed him. He lies in the wood, there is snow on the ground, crows caw, squirrels leap. I like squirrels. That poor gentleman in his fine overcoat lies dead, not far from his car. I can drive a car. I love violets and music. I was born at Zwickau. My father was a bald-headed bespectacled shoemaker, and my mother was a washerwoman with scarlet hands. When she used to get angry—

And all over again from the beginning, with new absurd details. . . . Thus, a reflected image, asserting itself, laid its claims. Not I sought a refuge in a foreign land, not I grew a beard, but Felix, my slayer. Ah, if I had known him well, for years of intimacy, I might even have found it amusing to take up new quarters in the soul I had inherited. I would have known every cranny in it; all the corridors of its past; I could have enjoyed the use of all its accommodations. But Felix's soul I had studied very cursorily, so that all I knew of it were the bare outlines of his personality, two or three chance traits. Should I practice doing things with my left hand?

Such sensations, however nasty, were possible to deal with —more or less. It was, for example, rather hard to forget how utterly he had surrendered himself to me, that soft-stuffed creature, when I was getting him ready for his execution. Those cold obedient paws! It quite bewildered me to recall how pliant he had been. His toenail was so strong that my scissors could not bite in at once, it screwed round one blade as the jag of a tin of corned beef envelops the key. Is a man's will really so powerful as to be able to convert another into a dummy? Did I actually shave him? Astounding! Yes, what tormented me above all, when recalling things, was Felix's submissiveness, the ridiculous, brainless, automatous quality of his submissiveness. But, as said already, I got over that. Far worse was my failure to put up with mirrors. In fact, the beard I started growing was meant to hide me not so much from others as from my own self. Dreadful thing— a hypertrophied imagination. So it is quite easy to understand that a man endowed with my acute sensitiveness gets into the devil of a state about such trifles as a reflection in a dark looking glass, or his own shadow, falling dead at his feet, *und so weiter.* Stop short, you people—I raise a huge white palm like a German policeman, stop! No sighs of compassion, people, none whatever. Stop, pity! I do not accept your sympathy; for among you there are sure to be a few souls who will pity me—me, a poet misunderstood. "Mist, vapor ... in the mist a chord that quivers." No, that's not verse, that's from old Dusty's great book, *Crime and Slime.* Sorry: *Schuld und Sühne* (German edition). Any remorse on my part is absolutely out of the question: an artist feels no remorse, even when his work is not understood, not accepted. As to that premium—

I know, I know: it is a bad mistake from the novelist's point of view that in the whole course of my tale there is— as far as I remember—so very little attention devoted to what seems to have been my leading motive; greed of gain. How does it come that I am so reticent and vague about the purpose I pursued in arranging to have a dead double? But here I am assailed by odd doubts: was I really so very, very much bent upon making profit and did it really seem to me so desirable, that rather equivocal sum (the worth of a man in terms of money; and a reasonable remuneration for his disappearance), or was it the other way round and remembrance, writing for me, could not (being truthful to the end) act otherwise and attach any special importance to a talk in Orlovius's study (did I describe that study?).

And there is one other thing I would like to say about my posthumous moods: although in my soul of souls I had no qualms about the perfection of my work, believing that in the black and white wood there lay a dead man perfectly resembling me, yet as a novice of genius, still unfamiliar with the flavor of fame, but filled with the pride that escorts self-stringency, I longed, to the point of pain, for that masterpiece of mine (finished and signed on the ninth of March in a gloomy wood) to be appreciated by men, or in other words, for the deception—and every work of art is a deception—to act successfully; as to the royalties, so to speak, paid by the insurance firm, that was in my mind a matter of secondary importance. Oh, yes, I was the pure artist of romance.

Things that pass are treasured later, as the poet sang. One fine day at last Lydia joined me abroad; I called at her hotel. "Not so wildly," I said with grave warning, as she was about to fling herself into my arms. "Remember that my name is Felix, and that I am merely an acquaintance of yours." She looked very comely in her widow's weeds, just as my artistic black bow and nicely trimmed beard suited me. She began relating ... yes, everything had worked as I had expected, without a hitch. It appeared she had wept quite sincerely during the crematory service, when the pastor with a professional catch in his throbbing voice had spoken about me, "... and *this* man, *this* noblehearted man, who—" I imparted to her my further plans and very soon began to court her.

We are married now, I and my little widow; we live in a quiet picturesque place, in our cottage. We spend long lazy hours in the little myrtle garden with its view of the blue gulf far below, and talk very often of my poor dead brother. I keep recounting to her new episodes from his life. "Fate, kismet," says Lydia with a sigh. "At least now, in Heaven, his soul is consoled by our being happy."

Yes, Lydia is happy with me; she needs nobody else. "How glad I am," she says sometimes, "that we are forever rid of Ardalion. I used to pity him a good deal, and gave him a lot of my time, but, really, I could never stand the man. Wonder where he is at present. Probably drinking himself to death, poor fellow. That's also fate!"

In the mornings I read and write; maybe I shall soon publish one or two little things under my new name; a Russian author who lives in the neighborhood highly praises my style and vivid imagination.

Occasionally Lydia receives a line from Orlovius—New Year's greetings, say. He invariably asks her to give his kindest regards to her husband whom he has not the pleasure of knowing, and probably thinks the while: "Ah, here is a widow who is easily comforted. Poor Hermann Karlovich!"

Do you feel the tang of this epilogue? I have concocted it according to a classic recipe. Something is told about every character in the book to wind up the tale; and in doing so, the dribble of their existence is made to remain correctly, though summarily, in keeping with what has been previously shown of their respective ways; also, a facetious note is admitted—poking sly fun at life's conservativeness.

Lydia is as forgetful and untidy as ever. . . .

And left to the very end of the epilogue there is, *pour la bonne bouche,* some especially hearty bit, quite possibly having to do with an insignificant object which just flicked by in some earlier part of the novel:

You may still see on the wall of their chamber the same pastel portrait, and as usual, whenever he looks at it, Hermann laughs and curses.

Finis. Farewell, Turgy! Fairwell, Dusty!

Dreams, dreams . . . and rather trite ones at that. Who cares, anyway? . . .

Let us return to our tale. Let us try to control ourselves better. Let us omit certain details of the journey. I remember that when I arrived at Pignan, almost on the Spanish border, the first thing I did was to try and obtain German newspapers; I did find a few, but there was nothing in them yet.

I took a room in a second-rate hotel, a huge room, with a stone floor and walls like cardboard, on which there seemed to be painted the sienna-brown door leading into the next room, and a looking glass with only one reflection. It was horribly cold; yet the open hearth of the preposterous fireplace was no more adapted to give heat than a stage contrivance would be, and when the chips brought by the maid had burned out, the room seemed colder still. The night I spent there was full of the most extravagant and exhausting visions; and as morning came, and feeling sticky and prickly all over, I emerged into the narrow street, inhaled the sickening rich odors and was crushed among the southern crowd jostling in the marketplace, it became quite clear to me that I simply could not remain in that town any longer.

With shivers continuously running down my spine and a head fairly bursting, I made my way to the *syndicat d'initiative,* where a talkative individual suggested a score of resorts in the vicinity: I wanted a cosy secluded one, and when toward evening a leisurely bus dropped me at the address

I had chosen, it struck me that here was exactly what I desired.

Apart, alone, surrounded by cork oaks, stood a decent-looking hotel, the greater part still shuttered (the season beginning only in summer). A strong wind from Spain worried the chick fluff of the mimosas. In a pavilion, reminding one of a chapel, a spring of curative water gushed, and cobwebs hung in the corners of its ruby dark windows.

Few people were staying there. There was the doctor, the soul of the hotel and the sovereign of the table d'hôte: he sat at the head of the table and did the talking; there was the parrot-beaked old fellow in the alpaca coat, who used to produce an assortment of snorts and grunts, when, with a light patter of feet, the nimble maid served the trout which he had angled in the neighboring stream; there was a vulgar young couple come to this hole all the way from Madagascar; there was the little old lady in the muslin *gorgerette,* a school mistress; there was a jeweler with a large family; there was a finicking young person, who was styled at first vicomtesse, then comtesse and finally (which brings us to the time I am writing this) marquise—all due to the doctor's exertions (who does all he can to enhance the establishment's reputation). Let us not forget, too, the mournful commercial traveler from Paris, representative of a patented species of ham; nor the coarse fat abbé who kept jawing about the beauty of some cloister in the vicinity; and, to express it better, he would pluck a kiss from his meaty lips pursed into the semblance of a heartlet. That was all the collection, I believe. The beetle-browed manager stood near the door with his hands clasped behind his back and followed with a surly eye the ceremonial dinner. Outside a riotous wind raged.

These novel impressions had a beneficial effect upon me. The food was good. I had a sunny room, and it was interesting to watch, from the window, the wind roughly upturning the several petticoats of the olive trees which it tumbled. In the distance against a mercilessly blue sky, there stood out the mauve-shaded sugar cone of a mountain resembling Fujiyama. I was not much out of doors: it frightened me, that thunder in my head, that incessant crashing, blinding March wind, that murderous mountain draft. Still, on the second day, I went to town for newspapers, and once again there was nothing in them, and because the suspense exasperated me beyond measure, I determined not to trouble about them for a few days.

The impression I made upon the table d'hôte was, I am afraid, one of gruff unsociability, although I tried hard to answer all questions addressed to me; but in vain did the doctor press me to go to the *salon* after dinner, a stuffy little room with a cottage piano out of tune, plush armchairs and a round table littered with touring advertisements. The doctor had a goat's beard, watery blue eyes and a round little belly. He fed in a businesslike and very disgusting manner. His method of dealing with poached eggs was to give the yolk an underhand twist with a crust of bread which landed it whole, to the accompaniment of a juicy intake of saliva, into his wet, pink mouth. He used to gather, with gravy-soaked fingers, the bones left after the meat course on people's plates, and wrap up his spoil anyhow, and thrust it into the pocket of his ample coat; by doing so he evidently aimed at being taken for an eccentric character: "*C'est pour les pauvres chiens,* for the poor dogs," he would say (and says so still), "animals are often better than human beings"—an affirmation that provoked (and goes on doing so) passionate disputes, the abbé waxing especially hot. Upon learning that I was a German and a musician the doctor seemed quite fas-

cinated; and from the glances directed at me, I concluded
that it was not so much my face (on its way from unshaven-
ness to beardedness) which attracted attention, as my nation-
ality and profession, in both of which the doctor perceived
something distinctly favorable to the prestige of the house.
He would buttonhole me on the stairs or in one of the long
white passages, and start upon some endless gossiping, now
discussing the social faults of the ham deputy, then deploring
the abbé's intolerance. It was all getting a little upon my
nerves, although diverting after a fashion.

As soon as night fell and the shadows of branches, which
a solitary lamp in the courtyard caught and lost, came sweeping across my room, a sterile and hideous confusion filled
my vast vacant soul. Oh, no, I have never feared dead bodies,
just as broken, shattered playthings do not frighten me. What
I feared, all alone in a treacherous world of reflections, was
to break down instead of holding on till a certain extraordinary, madly happy, all-solving moment which it was
imperative I should attain; the moment of an artist's triumph;
of pride, deliverance, bliss: was my picture a sensational success or was it a dismal flop?

On the sixth day of my stay the wind became so violent
that the hotel could be likened to a ship at sea in a tempest:
windowpanes boomed, walls creaked; and the heavy evergreen foliage fell back with a receding rustle and then lurch-
ing forward, stormed the house. I attempted to go out into
the garden, but at once was doubled up, retained my hat by
a miracle and went up to my room. Once there, standing deep
in thought at the window amid all that turmoil and tin-
tinnabulation I failed to hear the gong, so that when I came
down to lunch and took my seat at the table, the third course
was in progress—giblets, mossy to the palate, with tomato

sauce—the doctor's favorite dish. At first I did not heed the
general conversation, skillfully guided by the doctor, but all
of a sudden noticed that everyone was gazing at me.

"*Et vous*—and you," the doctor was saying to me, "what
do you think upon this subject?"

"What subject?" I asked.

"We were speaking," said the doctor, "of that murder,
*chez vous,* in Germany. What a monster a man must be"—
he went on, anticipating an interesting discussion—"to insure
his life and then take another's—"

I do not know what came over me, but suddenly I lifted
my hand and said: "Look here, stop," and, bringing it down,
with my clenched fist I gave the table a bang that made the
napkin ring jump into the air, and I cried, in a voice which
I did not recognize as mine: "Stop, stop! How dare you,
what right have you got? Of all the insulting— No, I won't
stand it! How dare you— Of my land, of my people . . . be
silent! Be silent," I cried ever louder: "You! . . . To dare tell
me to my face that in Germany— Be silent!"

As it was, they had all been silent for a long time already
—since that moment when, from the bang of my fist, the
ring had started rolling. It rolled to the very end of the
table; and was cautiously tapped down by the jeweler's
youngest son. A silence of exceptionally fine quality. Even the
wind, I believe, had ceased booming. The doctor, holding his
knife and fork, froze: a fly froze on his forehead. I felt a
spasm in my throat; I threw down my napkin and left the
dining room, with every face automatically turning to watch
me pass.

Without pausing in my stride I grabbed the newspaper
that lay outspread on a table in the hall and, once in my
room, sank down upon my bed. I was trembling all over,

strangled by rising sobs, convulsed with fury; my knuckles were filthily splashed with tomato sauce. As I pored over the paper I still had time to tell myself that it was all nonsense, a mere coincidence—one could hardly expect Frenchmen to hear of the matter, but in a flash my name, my former name, came dancing before my eyes. . . .

I do not recall exactly what I learned from that particular paper: since then I have perused heaps of them, and they have got rather mixed up in my mind; they are now lying somewhere about, but I have not the leisure to sort them. What I well remember, however, was that I immediately grasped two facts: first, that the murderer's identity was known, and second, that that of the victim was not. The communication did not proceed from a special correspondent, but was merely a brief summary of what, presumably, the German papers contained, and there was something careless and in-solent about the fashion in which it was served up, between reports of a political fray and a case of psittacosis. And I was unspeakably shocked by the tone of the thing: it was in fact so improper, so impossible in regard to me, that for a moment I even thought it might refer to a person bearing the same name as I; for such a tone is used when writing of some half-wit hacking to bits a whole family. I understand now. It was, I guess, a ruse on the part of the international police; a silly attempt to frighten and rattle me; but not realizing this, I was, at first, in a frenzy of passion, and spots swam before my eyes which kept blundering into this or that line of the column—when suddenly there came a loud knock at the door. I shoved the paper under my bed and said: "Come in."

It was the doctor. He was finishing chewing something. *"Ecoutez,"* he said, having hardly crossed the threshold—

"there has been a mistake. You have wrongly interpreted my meaning. I'd very much like—"

"Out!"—I roared—"out you go!"

His face changed and he went without closing the door. I jumped up and slammed it with an incredible crash. Then, from under the bed, I pulled out the paper; but now I could not find in it what I had just been reading. I examined it from beginning to end: nothing! Could I have *dreamt* reading it? I started looking through the pages afresh; it was like a nightmare when a thing gets lost, and not only can it not be discovered but there are none of those natural laws which would lend the search a certain logic, instead of which everything is absurdly shapeless and arbitrary. No, there was nothing about me in the paper. Nothing at all. I must probably have been in an awful state of blind excitement, because a few seconds later I noticed that the paper was an old German rag and not the Paris one which I had been reading. Diving under the bed again I retrieved it and reread the trivially worded, and even libelous, communication. Now it dawned upon me what had shocked me most—shocked me as an insult: not a word was there about our resemblance; not only was it not criticized (for instance they might have said, at least: "Yes, an admirable resemblance, yet such and such markings show it to be not his body") but it was not mentioned at all—which left one with the impression that it was some wretch whose appearance was quite different from mine. Now, one single night could not very well have decomposed him; on the contrary his countenance ought to have acquired a marble quality, making our likeness still more sharply chiseled; but even if the body had been found quite a few days later, thus giving playful Death time to tamper with it, all the same the stages of its decomposition would have tallied with mine—damned hasty way of putting it, I am afraid, but I am in no mood for niceties. This affected ignorance of what, to me, was most precious and all-important, struck me as an extremely cowardly trick, implying as it did that, from the very first, everybody knew perfectly well that it was not I, that it simply could not have entered anybody's head to mistake the corpse for mine. And the slipshod way in which the story was told seemed, in itself, to stress a solecism which I could certainly never, never have committed; and still there they were, mouths hidden, and snouts turned away, silent, but all aquiver, the ruffians, bubbling over with joy, yes, with an evil vindictive joy; yes, vindictive, jeering, unbearable—

Again there came a knock; I sprang to my feet, gasping. The doctor and the manager appeared. *"Voilà,"* said the doctor in a deeply hurt voice addressing the manager and pointing at me. "There—that gentleman not only took offense at something I never said, but has now insulted me, refusing to hear me out and being extremely rude. Will you please talk to him. I am not used to such manners."

*"Il faut s'expliquer*—you must thrash it out," said the manager glowering at me darkly. "I'm sure that monsieur himself—"

"Be gone!" I yelled, stamping my foot. "The things you are doing to me— It's beyond— You dare not humiliate me and take revenge— I demand, do you hear, I demand—" The doctor and the manager, both with raised palms and in clockwork style prancing on stiff legs, started gibbering at me, strutting ever closer; I could not stand it any longer, my fit of passion passed, but in its stead I felt the pressure of tears, and suddenly (leaving victory to whoever sought it) I fell upon my bed and sobbed violently.

"Nerves, just nerves," said the doctor, softening as if by magic.

The manager smiled and left the room, closing the door with great gentleness. The doctor poured out a glass of water for me, offered to bring a soothing drug, stroked my shoulder; and I sobbed on and was perfectly conscious of my condition, even saw with cold mocking lucidity its shame, and at the same time I felt all the Dusty-and-Dusky charm of hysterics and also something dimly advantageous to me, so I continued to shake and heave, as I wiped my cheeks with the large, dirty meat-smelling handkerchief which the doctor gave me, while he patted me and muttered soothingly:

"Only a misunderstanding! *Moi, qui dis toujours . . .* I, with my usual saying that we've had our fill of wars . . . You've got your defects, and we've got ours. Politics should be forgotten. You've simply not understood what we were talking about. I was simply inquiring what you thought of that murder. . . ."

"What murder?" I asked through my sobs.

"Oh, *une sale affaire*—a beastly business: changed clothes with a man and killed him. But appease yourself, my friend, it is not only in Germany that murderers exist, we have our Landrus, thank heaven, so that you are not alone. *Calmez-vous,* it is all nerves, the local water acts beautifully upon the nerves—or more exactly, upon the stomach, *ce qui revient au même, d'ailleurs.*"

He went on with his patter for a little while and then rose. I returned the handkerchief with thanks.

"Know what?" he said when already standing in the doorway. "The little countess is quite infatuated with you. So you ought to play us something on the piano tonight" (he ran his fingers in the semblance of a trill) "and believe me you'll have her in your beddy."

He was practically in the passage, but all at once changed his mind and came back.

"In the days of my youth and folly," he said, "when we students were once making merry, the most blasphemous fellow among us got especially tight, so as soon as he reached the helpless stage, we dressed him up in a cassock, shaved a round patch on his pate and late at night knocked at the door of a cloister, whereupon a nun appeared and one of us said to her: *'Ah, ma soeur, voyez dans quel triste état s'est mis ce pauvre abbé*—see this poor priest's sorry condition! Take him, let him sleep it off in one of your cells.' And fancy, the nuns took him. What a laugh we had!" The doctor lowered his haunches slightly and slapped them. The thought suddenly occurred to me that, who knows, maybe he was saying all this (disguised him . . . wanted him to pass for someone else) with a certain secret design, that maybe he was sent to spy . . . and again fury possessed me, but glancing at his foolishly beaming wrinkles, I controlled myself, pretended to laugh; he waved his hands very contentedly and at last, at last, left me in peace.

In spite of a grotesque resemblance to Rascalnikov— No, that's wrong. Canceled. What came next? Yes, I decided that the very first thing to do was to obtain as many newspapers as possible. I ran downstairs. On one of the landings I happened upon the fat abbé, who looked at me with commiseration: from his oily smile I deduced that the doctor had already managed to tell the world of our reconciliation.

Coming out into the court I was at once half stunned by the wind; I did not give in, though, but clapped myself eagerly against the gate, and then the bus appeared, I signaled

to it, I climbed in and we rolled down hill with the white
dust madly whirling. In town I got several German dailies
and took the occasion to call at the post office. There was no
letter for me, but, on the other hand, I found the papers full
of news, much too full, alas. . . . Today after a week of all-
absorbing literary labor, I am cured and feel only contempt,
but at the time the cold sneering tone of the Press almost
drove me crazy.

Here is the general picture I finally put together: on Sunday noon, the tenth of March, in a wood, a hairdresser from
Koenigsdorf found a dead body. How he came to be in that
wood, which, even in summer, remained unfrequented, and
why it was only in the evening that he made his find known,
are puzzles still unsolved. Next follows that screamingly funny
story which I have, I think, mentioned already: the car purposely left by me on the border of the wood was gone. Its
imprints, a succession of T's, established the make of the tires,
while certain Koenigsdorf inhabitants possessing phenomenal
memories recollected having seen a blue Icarus pass, small
model, wire wheels, to which the bright and pleasant fellows at the garage in my street added information concerning
horsepower and cylinders, and gave not only the car's police
number, but also the factory one of engine and chassis.

The general assumption is that at this very instant I am
spinning about in that Icarus somewhere—which is deliciously
ludicrous. Now, it is obvious to me, that somebody saw my
car from the highway and, without further ado, appropriated
it, overlooking in his hurry, the corpse lying close by.

Inversely, that hairdresser who did notice the corpse asserts
that there was no car around whatsoever. He is a suspicious
character, that man! It would seem to be the most natural
thing in the world for the police to pounce upon him; people

have had their heads chopped off for less, but you may be sure that nothing of the sort has happened, they do not dream of seeing in him the possible murderer; no, the guilt has been laid upon me, straightaway, unreservedly, with cold and callous promptitude, as though they were joyfully eager to convict me, as though it were vengeance, as though I had long been offending them and they had long been thirsting to punish me. Not only taking for granted, with strange prejudication, that the dead man could not be I; not only failing to observe our resemblance, but, as it were, *a priori,* excluding its possibility (for people do not see what they are loath to see), the police gave a brilliant example of logic when they expressed their surprise at my having hoped to deceive the world simply by dressing up in my clothes an individual who was not in the least like me. The imbecility and blatant unfairness of such reasoning are highly comic. The next logical step was to make me mentally deficient; they even went so far as to suppose I was not quite sane and certain persons knowing me confirmed this—that ass Orlovius among others (wonder who the others were), his story being that I used to write letters to myself (rather unexpected).

What baffled the police absolutely, was the question how did my victim (the word "victim" was particularly relished by the Press) come to be in my clothes, or better, say, how had I managed to force a live man to put on not only my suit, but down to my socks and shoes, which being too small for him ought to have hurt—(well, as to shoeing him, I could have done that post-factum, wise guys!)

In getting into their heads that it was not my corpse, they behaved just as a literary critic does, who at the mere sight of a book by an author whom he does not favor, makes up his mind that the book is worthless and thence proceeds to build whatever he wants to build, on the basis of that first gratuitous assumption. Thus, faced by the miracle of Felix's resemblance to me, they hurled themselves upon such small and quite immaterial blemishes as would, given a deeper and finer attitude towards my masterpiece, pass unnoticed, the way a beautiful book is not in the least impaired by a misprint or a slip of the pen. They mentioned the roughness of the hands, they even sought out some horny growth of the gravest significance, noting, nevertheless, the neatness of the nails on all four extremities; and somebody—to the best of my belief, that hairdresser who found the body—drew the sleuths' attention to the fact that on the strength of certain details visible to a professional (lovely, that) it was clear that the nails had been pared by an expert—which ought to have inculpated *him* and not me!

Try as I may, I cannot find out what was Lydia's demeanor at the inquest. As none doubted that the murdered man was not I, she has certainly been, or still is, suspected of complicity: her own fault to be sure—ought to have understood that the insurance money had faded into thin air, so no use butting in with widow's wailings. She will break down in the long run, and never questioning my innocence but striving to save my head, will give away my brother's tragic story; to no avail, however, for it may be established without much difficulty that I never had any brother; and as to the suicide theory, well, there is hardly any chance of the official imagination swallowing that trigger-and-string stunt.

Of the greatest importance to my present security is the fact that the murdered man's identity is unknown and *cannot* be known. Meanwhile I have been living under his name, traces of which I have already left here and there, so that I might be run to earth in no time were it discovered *whom*

I have, to use the accepted term, plugged. But there is no way of discovering it, which suits me admirably, as I am too tired to plan and act all over again. And, indeed, how could I divest myself of a name, which, with such art I have made my own? For I look like my name, gentlemen, and it fits me as exactly as it used to fit him. You must be fools not to understand.

Now as to that car, it ought to be found sooner or later—not that it will help them much; for I *wanted* it to be found. What fun! They think I am meekly sitting at the wheel, whereas, actually, they will find a very ordinary and very scared thief.

I make no mention here of the monstrous epithets which those irresponsible scribblers, those purveyors of thrills, those villainous quacks who set up their stalls where blood has been spilt, consider it necessary to award me; neither shall I dwell upon the solemn arguments of a psychoanalytic kind in which writers-up rejoice. All that drivel and dirt incensed me at the outset, especially the fact of my being associated with this or that oaf with vampirish tastes, who, in his day, had helped to raise the number of sold copies. There was, for instance, that fellow who burned his car with his victim's body inside, after having wisely sawed off part of the feet, as the corpse had turned out to exceed in length his, the car owner's, measure. But to hell with them! They and I have nothing in common. Another point that maddened me was that the papers printed my passport photo (on which I indeed look like a criminal, and not like myself at all, so maliciously did they touch it up) instead of some other one, that one, say, where I dip into a book—an expensive affair in tender milk-chocolate shades; and the same photographer took me in another pose, finger at the temple, grave eyes looking up at you from under bent brows: that is the way German novelists like to be taken. Really, they had many to choose from. There are some good snapshots too—that one, for example, which depicts me in bathing shorts on Ardalion's plot of land.

Oh, by the way—almost forgot, the police during their careful investigations, examining every bush and even digging into the soil, discovered nothing; nothing, except one remarkable object, namely: a bottle—*the* bottle—of homemade vodka. It had been lying there since June: I have, as far as I recollect, described Lydia's hiding it. . . . Pity I didn't bury a balalaika somewhere too, so as to give them the pleasure of imagining a Slavic murder to the clinking of goblets and the singing of *"Pazhaláy zhemen-áh, dara-gúy-ah. . . ."* "Do take pity of me, dear. . . ."

But enough, enough. All that disgusting mess is due to the inertia, pigheadedness, prejudice of humans, failing to recognize me in the corpse of my flawless double. I accept, with a feeling of bitterness and contempt, the bare fact of unrecognition (whose mastery was not darkened by it?) but I keep on firmly believing in my double's perfection. I have nothing to blame myself for. Mistakes—pseudo mistakes—have been imposed upon me retrospectively by my critics when they jumped to the groundless conclusion that my very idea was radically wrong, thereupon picking out those trifling discrepancies, which I myself am aware of and which have no importance whatever in the sum of an artist's success. I maintain that in the planning and execution of the whole thing the limit of skill was attained; that its perfect finish was, in a sense, inevitable; that all came together, regardless of my will, by means of creative intuition. And so, in order to obtain recognition, to justify and save the offspring of my brain, to explain to the world all the depth of my master-piece, did I devise the writing of the present tale.

For, after crumpling and flinging aside one last newspaper, having sucked it dry, learned everything; with a burning, itching sensation creeping over me, and an intense desire to adopt at once certain measures I alone could appreciate; it was then, in that state, that I sat down at my table and began to write. If I were not absolutely certain of my literary forces, of the remarkable knack—at first it was tough, uphill business. I panted and stopped and then went on again. My toil, mightily wearing me out, gave me a queer delight. Yes, a drastic remedy, an inhuman, medieval purge; but it proved efficient.

Since the day I began a full week has gone by; and now my work is nearing its end. I am calm. Everyone at the hotel is beautifully nice to me; the treacle of affability. At present I take my meals separately, at a little table near the window. The doctor approves of my separation, and heedless of my being within earshot he explains to people that a nervous subject requires peace and that as a rule musicians are nervous subjects. During meals he frequently addresses me across the room from the top of the table d'hôte recommending some dish or else jokingly asking me whether I could not be tempted to join in the general repast just only for today, and then they all glance over at me in a most good-natured fashion.

But how tired I am, how deadly tired. There have been days, the day before yesterday for instance—when, except for two short interruptions, I wrote nineteen hours at a stretch; and do you suppose I slept after that? No, I could not sleep, and my whole body strained and snapped as if I were being broken on the wheel. Now, however, when I am finishing and have almost nothing more to add to my tale, it is quite a wrench to part with all this used-up paper; but part with it I must; and after reading my work over again, correcting it, sealing it up and bravely posting it, I shall have, I suppose, to move on farther, to Africa, to Asia—does not much matter whither—though I am so reluctant to move, so desirous of quietude. Indeed, let the reader only imagine the position of a man living under a certain name, not because he cannot obtain another passp—

# Chapter Eleven

I have moved to a slightly higher altitude: disaster made me shift my quarters.

I thought there would be ten chapters in all—my mistake! It is odd to remember how firmly, how composedly, in spite of everything, I was bringing the tenth one to a close; which I did not quite manage—and happened to break my last paragraph on a rhyme to "gasp." The maid bustled in to make up my room, so having nothing better to do, I went down into the garden; and there a heavenly, soft stillness enfolded me. At first I did not even realize what was the matter, but I shook myself and suddenly understood, the hurricane wind which had been raging lately was stilled.

The air was divine, there drifted about the silky floss of sallows; even the greenery of indeciduous leafage tried to look renovated; and the half-bared, athletic torsos of the cork oaks glistened a rich red.

I strolled along the main road; on my right, the swarthy vineyards slanted, their still naked shoots standing in uniform pattern and looking like crouching, crooked cemetery crosses. Presently I sat down on the grass, and as I looked across the vineyards at the golden gorse-clad top of a hill, which was up to its shoulders in thick oak foliage, and at the deep-deep blue-blue sky, I reflected with a kind of melting tenderness (for perhaps the essential, though hidden, feature of my soul is tenderness) that a new simple life had started, leaving the burden of laborious fantasies behind. Then, afar, from the direction of my hotel, the motorbus appeared and I decided to amuse myself for the very last time with reading Berlin papers. Once in the bus, I feigned to sleep (and pushed that performance to smiling in my dream), because I noticed, among the passengers, the commercial traveler in ham; but soon I fell asleep authentically.

Having obtained what I wanted in town, I opened the newspaper only when I got back, and with a good-humored chuckle settled down to its perusal. All at once I laughed outright: the car had been discovered.

Its vanishing received the following explanation: three boon companions walking, on the morning of the tenth of March, along the highway—an unemployed mechanic, the hairdresser we already know, and the hairdresser's brother, a youth with no fixed occupation—espied on the distant fringe of the forest the gleam of a car's radiator and incontinently made towards it. The hairdresser, a staid, law-abiding man, then said that one ought to wait for the owner and, if he did not turn up, drive the car to the police station at Koenigsdorf, but his brother and the mechanic, both liking a bit of fun, had another suggestion to make. The hairdresser retorted, however, that he would not allow anything of the sort; and he went deeper into the wood, looking about him as he did so. Soon he came upon the corpse. He hurried back, halloing for his comrades, and was horrified at not finding either them or the car. For some time he loitered about, thinking they might return. They did not. Towards evening he at last made up his mind to inform the police of his "gruesome discovery," but, being a loving brother, he said nothing about the car.

What transpired now was that those two scamps had soon damaged my Icarus, which they eventually hid, intending to lie low themselves, but then thought better of it and surrendered. "In the car"—the report added—"an object was found settling the murdered man's identity."

First, by a slip of the eye, I read "the murderer's identity" and this increased my hilarity, for was it not known from the very beginning that the car belonged to me? But a second reading set me thinking.

That phrase irritated me. There was some silly huggermugger about it. Of course, I at once told myself that either it was some new catch, or else they had found something of no more importance than that ridiculous vodka. Still, it worried me—and for a while I was conscientious enough to check in my mind all the articles that had taken part in the affair (I even remembered the rag he used for a handkerchief and his revolting comb) and as I had acted at the time with sharp and sure accuracy, I now had no difficulty in working back and was satisfied to find everything in order. Q.E.D.

In vain: I had no peace. . . . It was high time to get that last chapter finished, but instead of writing I went out of doors again, roaming till late, and when I returned, I was so utterly fagged out, that sleep overcame me at once, despite the confused discomfort of my mind. I dreamt that after a tedious search (offstage—not shown in my dream) I at last found Lydia, who was hiding from me and who now coolly declared that all was well, she had got the inheritance all right and was going to marry another man, "because, you see," she said, "you are dead." I woke up in a terrific rage, my heart pounding madly: fooled! helpless!—for how could a dead man sue the living—yes, helpless—and she knew it! Then I came to my wits again and laughed—what humbugs dreams are liable to be. But of a sudden I felt that there *was* something extremely disagreeable which no amount of laughing could do away with, and that it was not my dream that mattered—what really mattered was the mysteriousness of yesterday's news: the object found in the car . . . if indeed, I reflected, it is neither a wily snare nor a mare's nest; if, indeed, it has proved possible to find a name for the murdered party, and if that name is the right one. No, there were too many ifs; I recalled the carefulness of yesterday's test when I followed up the curves, graceful and regular as the paths of planets, which the diverse objects used had taken—oh, I could have dotted out their orbits! But nevertheless my mind remained ill at ease.

In quest of some way of freeing myself of those intolerable forebodings I gathered the sheets of my manuscript, weighed the lot on my palm, even muttered a facetious "well, well!" and decided that before penning the two or three final sentences I would read it over from beginning to end.

It struck me that a great treat was now in store for me. Standing in my nightshirt near the writing table, it was lovingly that I shook down between my hands the rustling profusion of bescribbled pages. That done, I got into my bed once more; properly arranged the pillow under my shoulder blades; then noticed that I had left the manuscript lying on the table, although I could have sworn to its having been in my hands all along. Calmly, without cursing, I got up and brought it back with me into bed, propped up the pillow anew, glanced at the door, asked myself if it was locked or not (as I disliked the prospect of interrupting my reading in order to let in the maid when she would bring my breakfast at nine); got up again—and again quite calmly; satisfied myself that the door was not locked, so that I might have not bothered, cleared my throat, got back into my tumbled bed, settled down comfortably, was about to begin reading, but now my cigarette had gone out. In contrast with German brands, French cigarettes claim one's constant attention. Where had the matches vanished? Had them a moment ago! For the third time I got up, now with my hands trembling slightly; discovered the matches behind the inkpot—but upon returning into my bed squashed under my hip another boxful hiding in the bedclothes, which meant that I again might have spared myself the trouble of getting up. I lost my temper; collected the scattered sheets of my manuscript from the floor, and the delicious foretaste with which I had just been penetrated, now changed to something like pain—to a horrible apprehension, as if an evil imp were promising to disclose to me more and more blunders and nothing but blunders. Having, however, lit up my cigarette again and punched into submissiveness that shrewish pillow, I was able to set about my reading. What amazed me was the absence of title on the first leaf: for assuredly I *had* at one time invented a title, something beginning with "Memoirs of a—" of a what? I could not remember; and, anyway, "Memoirs" seemed dreadfully dull and commonplace. What should I call my book then? "The Double"? But Russian literature possessed one already. "Crime and Pun"? Not bad—a little crude, though. "The Mirror"? "Portrait of the Artist in a Mirror"? Too jejune, too *à la mode* ... what about "The Likeness"? "The Unrecognized Likeness"? "Justification of a Likeness"? No—dryish, with a touch of the philosophical. Something on the lines of "Only the Blind Do Not Kill"? Too long. Maybe: "An Answer to Critics"? or "The Poet and the Rabble"? Must think it over ... but first let us read the book, said I aloud, the title will come afterwards.

I began to read—and promptly found myself wondering whether I was reading written lines or seeing visions. Even more: my transfigured memory inhaled, as it were, a double dose of oxygen; my room was still lighter, because the panes had been washed; my past still more graphic, because twice irradiated by art. Once again I was climbing the hill near Prague—hearing the lark in the sky, seeing the round red dome of the gasworks; again in the grip of a tremendous emotion I stood over the sleeping tramp, and again he stretched his limbs and yawned, and again, dangling head down from his buttonhole, a limp little violet hung. I went on reading, and one by one they appeared: my rosy wife, Ardalion, Orlovius; and they all were alive, but in a certain sense I held their lives in my hands. Once again I looked at the yellow signpost, and walked through the wood with my mind already plotting; again on an autumn day my wife and I stood watching a leaf which fell to meet its reflection; and there was I myself, softly falling into a Saxon town full of strange repetitions, and there was my double softly rising to meet me. And again I wove my spell about him, and had him in my toils but he slipped away, and I feigned to give up my scheme, and with an unexpected potency the story blazed forth anew, demanding of its creator a continuation and an ending. And once again on a March afternoon I was dreamily driving along the highway, and there, in the ditch, near the post, he was waiting for me.

"Get in, quick, we must drive off."

"Where to?" he queried.

"Into that wood."

"There?" he asked and pointed—

With his stick, reader, with his stick. S-T-I-C-K, gentle reader. A roughly hewn stick branded with the owner's name:

Felix Wohlfahrt from Zwickau. With his stickau he pointed, gentle or lowly reader, with his stick! You know what a stick is, don't you? Well, that's what he pointed with—a stick— and got into the car, and left the stick there, upon getting out again, naturally—for the car temporarily belonged to him. I in fact noted that "quiet satisfaction." An artist's memory —what a curious thing! Beats all other kinds, I imagine. "There?"—he asked and pointed with his stick. Never in my life was I so astonished.

I sat in my bed and stared, pop-eyed, at the page, at the line written by me—sorry, not by me—but by that singular associate of mine: memory; and well did I see how irreparable it was. Not the fact of their finding his stick and so discovering our common name, which would now unavoidably lead to my capture—oh, no, not *that* galled me—but the thought that the whole of my masterpiece, which I had devised and worked out with such minute care, was now destroyed intrinsically, was turned into a little heap of mold, by reason of the mistake I had committed. Listen, listen! Even if his corpse *had* passed for mine, all the same they would have found that stick and then caught me, thinking they were pinching him— there is the greatest disgrace! For my whole construction had been based upon just the impossibility of a blunder, and now it appeared that a blunder there had been—and of the very grossest, drollest, tritest nature. Listen, listen! I bent over the shattered remains of my marvelous thing, and an accursed voice shrieked into my ear that the rabble which refused me recognition was perchance right. . . . Yes, I fell to doubting everything, doubting essentials, and I understood that what little life still lay before me would be solely devoted to a futile struggle against that doubt; and I smiled the smile of the condemned and in a blunt pencil that screamed with pain wrote swiftly and boldly on the first page of my work: "Despair"; no need to look for a better title.

The maid brought my coffee; I drank it, leaving the toast untouched. Then I hurriedly dressed, packed and carried my bag down myself. The doctor luckily did not see me. The manager showed surprise at my sudden departure and made me pay an exorbitant bill; but that did not matter to me any more: I was going away merely because it was *de rigueur* in such cases. I was following a certain tradition. Incidentally, I had grounds to presume that the French police were already on my scent.

On the way to town, I saw from my bus two policemen in a fast car which was white as a miller's back: they dashed by in the opposite direction and were gone in a burst of dust; but whether they were coming with the definite purpose of arresting me, that I could not say—and moreover, they may not have been policemen at all—no, I could not say—they passed much too rapidly. Upon arriving at Pignan I called at the post office, and now I am sorry I called, as I could have done perfectly without the letter I got there. On the same day I chose, at random, a landscape in a flamboyant booklet and late in the evening arrived here, at this mountain village. As to that letter . . . On second thought I had better copy it out, it is a fine sample of human malice.

"See here, I am writing to you, my good sir, for three reasons: (1) she asked me to do so; (2) my firm intention to tell you exactly what I think of you; (3) a sincere desire on my part to suggest your giving yourself up into the hands of the law, so as to clear up the bloody mess and disgusting mystery, from which she, innocent and terrified, suffers, of course, most. Let me warn you: it is with considerable doubt that

I regard all the dark Dostoevskian stuff you had taken the trouble to tell her. Putting it mildly, it is all a damned lie, I dare say. A damned cowardly lie, too, seeing the way you played on her feelings.

"She has asked me to write, because she thought you might still not know anything; she has quite lost her head and keeps saying you will get cross if one writes to you. I should very much like to see you getting cross now: it ought to be wildly funny.

". . . So that is how matters stand! It is not enough, however, to kill a man and clothe him adequately. A single additional detail is wanted and that is: resemblance between the two; but in the whole world there are not and cannot be, two men alike, however well you disguise them. True, any discussion of such subtleties was never even reached, since the very first thing the police told her was that a dead man with her husband's papers on him had been found, but that it was not her husband. And now comes the terrible part: being trained by a dirty cad, the poor little thing kept insisting, even before viewing the corpse (even before—does that come home to you?), insisting against all likelihood that it was her husband's body and none other's. I fail to grasp how on earth you managed to inspire a woman, who was and is practically a stranger to you, with such sacred awe. To achieve that, one ought to be, indeed, something out of the common in the way of monsters. God knows what an ordeal awaits her yet! It must not be. Your plain duty is to free her from that shade of complicity. Why, the case itself is clear to everybody! Those little tricks, my good man, with life policies, have been known for ages. I should even say that yours is the flattest and most hackneyed one of the lot.

"Next point: what I think of you. The first news reached me in a town where owing to meeting some fellow artists I happened to be stranded. You see, I never got as far as Italy—and I thank my stars I never did. Well, when I read that news, do you know what I felt? No surprise whatever! I have always known you to be a blackguard and a bully, and believe me, I did not keep back at the inquest all I had seen myself. So I described at length the treatment you gave her— your sneers and gibes and haughty contempt and nagging cruelty, and that chill of your presence which we all found so oppressive. You are wonderfully like a great grisly wild boar with putrid tusks—pity you did not put a roasted one into that suit of yours. And there is something else I want to get off my chest: whatever I may be—a weak-willed drunkard, or a chap ever ready to sell his honor for the sake of his art— let me tell you that I am ashamed of having accepted the morsels you flung me, and gladly would I publish my shame abroad, cry it out in the streets—if that might help to deliver me of its burden.

"See here, wild boar! This is a state of things that cannot endure. I want you to perish not because you are a killer, but because you are the meanest of mean scoundrels, using for your mean ends the innocence of a credulous young woman, whom, as it is, ten years of dwelling in your private hell have dazed and torn to pieces. If, nevertheless, there is still a chink in your blackness: give yourself up!"

I should leave this letter without any comments. The fairminded reader of my previous chapters could not have failed to note the genial tone, the kindliness of my attitude towards Ardalion; and that is how the man repaid me. But let it go, let it go. . . . Better to think he wrote that disgusting letter in his cups—otherwise it is really too much out of shape, too wide of truth, too full of libelous assertions, the absurdity of which will be easily seen by the same attentive reader. To call my gay, empty, and not very bright Lydia a "woman frightened out of her wits," or—what was his other expression?—"torn to pieces"; to hint at some kind of trouble between her and me, coming almost to cheek-slapping; really, really, that is a bit thick—I scarcely know in what words to describe it. There are no such words. My correspondent has already used them all up—though, true, in another connection. And just because I had of late been fondly supposing that I had passed the supreme limit of possible pain, injury, anxiety of mind, I now came into so dreadful a state whilst reading that letter over, such a fit of trembling possessed my body, that all things around me started shaking: the table; the tumbler on the table; even the mousetrap in a corner of my new room.

But suddenly I slapped my brow and burst out laughing. How simple it all was! How simply, said I to myself, the mysterious frenzy of that letter has now been solved. A proprietor's frenzy! Ardalion cannot forgive my having taken *his* name for cipher and staging the murder on *his* strip of earth. He is mistaken; all are gone bankrupt long ago; nobody knows whom this earth really belongs to—and . . . Ah, enough, enough about my fool Ardalion! The ultimate dab is laid on his portrait. With a last flourish of the brush I have signed it across the corner. It is a better thing than the nasty-colored death mask which that buffoon made of my face. Enough! A fine likeness, gentlemen.

And yet . . . How dare he? . . . Oh, go to the devil, go to the devil, all go to the devil!

March 31st. Night.

Alas, my tale degenerates into a diary. There is nothing to be done, though; for I have grown so used to writing, that now I am unable to desist. A diary, I admit, is the lowest form of literature. Connoisseurs will appreciate that lovely, self-conscious, falsely significant "Night" (meaning readers to imagine the sleepless variety of literary persons, so pale, so attractive). But as a matter of fact it *is* night at present.

The hamlet where I languish lies in the cradle of a dale, between tall close mountains. I have rented a large barnlike room in the house of a dusky old woman who has a grocer's shop below. The village consists of a single street. I might dwell at length on the charms of the spot, describing for instance the clouds that squeeze in and crawl through the house, using one set of windows, and then crawl out, using the opposite one—but it is a dull business describing such things. What amuses me is that I am the only tourist here; a foreigner to boot, and as folks have somehow managed to sniff out (oh, well, I suppose I told my landlady myself) that I came all the way from Germany, the curiosity I excite is unusual. Not since a film company came here a couple of seasons ago to take pictures of their starlet in *Les Contre-bandiers* has there been such excitement. Surely, I ought to hide myself, instead of which I get into the most conspicuous place; for it would be hard to find a brighter spotlight if that was the object. But I am dead-tired; the quicker it all ends, the better.

Today, most aptly, I made the acquaintance of the local gendarme—a perfectly farcical figure! Fancy a plumpish pink-faced individual, knock-kneed, wearing a black mustache.

I was sitting at the end of a street on a bench, and all around me villagers were being busy; or better say: were pretending to be busy; in reality they kept observing me with fierce inquisitiveness and no matter in what posture they happened to be—using every path of vision, across the shoulder, via the armpit, or from under the knee; I saw them at it quite clearly. The gendarme approached me with some diffidence; mentioned the rainy weather; passed on to politics and then to the arts. He even pointed out to me a scaffold of sorts painted yellow which was all that remained of the scene where one of the smugglers almost got hanged. He reminded me in some way of the late lamented Felix: that judicious note, that mother wit of the self-made man. I asked him when the last arrest had been effected in the place. He thought a bit and replied that it had been six years ago, when they took a Spaniard who had been pretty free with his knife during a brawl and then fled to the mountains. Anon my interlocutor found it necessary to inform me that in those mountains there existed bears which had been brought thither by man, to get rid of the indigenous wolves, which struck me as very comic. But *he* did not laugh; he stood there, with his right hand dejectedly twirling the left point of his mustache and proceeded to discuss modern education: "Now take me for example," he said. "I know geography, arithmetic, the science of war; I write a beautiful hand...." "And do you, perchance," I asked, "play the fiddle?" Sadly he shook his head.

At present, shivering in my icy room; cursing the barking dogs; expecting every minute to hear the guillotinette of the mousetrap in the corner crash down and behead an anonymous mouse; mechanically sipping the verbena infusion which my landlady considers it her duty to bring me, thinking I look seedy and fearing probably that I might die before the trial; at present, I say, I am sitting here and writing on this ruled paper—no other obtainable in the village—and then meditating, and then again glancing askance at the mousetrap. There is, thank God, no mirror in the room, no more than there is the God I am thanking. All is dark, all is dreadful, and I do not see any special reason for my lingering in the dark, vainly invented world. Not that I contemplate killing myself: it would be uneconomical—as we find in almost every country a person paid by the state to help a man lethally. And then the hollow hum of blank eternity. But the most remarkable thing, perhaps, is that there is a chance of it not ending yet, i.e., of their not executing me, but sentencing me to a spell of hard labor; in which case it may happen that in five years or so with the aid of some timely amnesty, I shall return to Berlin and manufacture chocolate all over again. I do not know why—but it sounds exceedingly funny.

Let us suppose, I kill an ape. Nobody touches me. Suppose it is a particularly clever ape. Nobody touches me. Suppose it is a new ape—a hairless, speaking species. Nobody touches me. By ascending these subtle steps circumspectly, I may climb up to Leibnitz or Shakespeare and kill them, and nobody will touch me, as it is impossible to say where the border was crossed, beyond which the sophist gets into trouble.

The dogs are barking. I am cold. That mortal inextricable pain . . . Pointed with his stick. Stick. What words can be twisted out of "stick"? Sick, tick, kit, it, is, ski, skit, sit. Abominably cold. Dogs barking: one of them begins and then all the others join in. It is raining. The electric lights here are wan, yellow. What on earth have I done?

## Chapter Eleven

April 1st.

The danger of my tale deteriorating into a lame diary is fortunately dispelled. Just now my farcical gendarme has been here: businesslike, wearing his saber; without looking into my eyes he politely asked to see my papers. I answered that it was all right, I would be dropping in one of these days, for police formalities, but that, at the moment, I did not care to get out of my bed. He insisted, was most civil, excused himself . . . had to insist. I got out of bed and gave him my passport. As he was leaving, he turned in the doorway and (always in the same polite voice) asked me to remain indoors. You don't say so!

I have crept up to the window and cautiously drawn the curtain aside. The street is full of people who stand there and gape; a hundred heads, I should say, gaping at my window. A dusty car with a policeman in it is camouflaged by the shade of the plane tree under which it discreetly waits. Through the crowd my gendarme edges his way. Better not look.

Maybe it is all mock existence, an evil dream; and presently I shall wake up somewhere; on a patch of grass near Prague. A good thing, at least, that they brought me to bay so speedily.

I have peeped again. Standing and staring. There are hundreds of them—men in blue, women in black, butcher boys, flower girls, a priest, two nuns, soldiers, carpenters, glaziers, postmen, clerks, shopkeepers . . . But absolute quiet; only the swish of their breathing. How about opening the window and making a little speech. . . .

"Frenchmen! This is a rehearsal. Hold those policemen. A famous film actor will presently come running out of this house. He is an arch-criminal but he must escape. You are asked to prevent them from grabbing him. This is part of the plot. French crowd! I want you to make a free passage for him from door to car. Remove its driver! Start the motor! Hold those policemen, knock them down, sit on them—we pay them for it. This is a German company, so excuse my French. *Les preneurs de vues*, my technicians and armed advisers are already among you. *Attention!* I want a clean getaway. That's all. Thank you. I'm coming out now."

Vladimir Nabokov was born in St. Petersburg on April 23, 1899. His family fled to Germany in 1919, during the Bolshevik Revolution. Nabokov studied French and Russian literature at Trinity College, Cambridge, from 1919 to 1923, then lived in Berlin (1923–1937) and Paris (1937–1940), where he began writing, mainly in Russian, under the pseudonym Sirin. In 1940 he moved to the United States, where he pursued a brilliant literary career (as a poet, novelist, critic, and translator) while teaching literature at Wellesley College, Stanford, Cornell, and Harvard. The monumental success of his novel *Lolita* (1955) enabled him to give up teaching and devote himself fully to his writing. In 1961 he moved to Montreux, Switzerland, where he died in 1977. Recognized as one of this century's master prose stylists in both Russian and English, he translated a number of his original English works—including *Lolita*—into Russian, and collaborated on English translations of his original Russian works.

# VINTAGE INTERNATIONAL

| | | |
|---|---|---|
| ___ Passions of the Mind by A.S. Byatt | $12.00 | 0-679-73678-6 |
| ___ Possession by A.S. Byatt | $12.00 | 0-679-73590-9 |
| ___ Sugar and Other Stories by A.S. Byatt | $10.00 | 0-679-74227-1 |
| ___ The Virgin in the Garden by A.S. Byatt | $12.00 | 0-679-73829-0 |
| ___ The Marriage of Cadmus and Harmony<br>by Roberto Calasso | $13.00 | 0-679-73348-5 |
| ___ Six Memos for the Next Millennium<br>by Italo Calvino | $10.00 | 0-679-74237-9 |
| ___ Exile and the Kingdom by Albert Camus | $10.00 | 0-679-73385-X |
| ___ The Fall by Albert Camus | $9.00 | 0-679-72022-7 |
| ___ The Myth of Sisyphus and Other Essays<br>by Albert Camus | $9.00 | 0-679-73373-6 |
| ___ The Plague by Albert Camus | $10.00 | 0-679-72021-9 |
| ___ The Rebel by Albert Camus | $11.00 | 0-679-73384-1 |
| ___ The Stranger by Albert Camus | $8.00 | 0-679-72020-0 |
| ___ Answered Prayers by Truman Capote | $10.00 | 0-679-75182-3 |
| ___ Breakfast at Tiffany's by Truman Capote | $10.00 | 0-679-74565-3 |
| ___ The Grass Harp by Truman Capote | $10.00 | 0-679-74557-2 |
| ___ In Cold Blood by Truman Capote | $12.00 | 0-679-74558-0 |
| ___ Music for Chameleons by Truman Capote | $11.00 | 0-679-74566-1 |
| ___ Other Voices, Other Rooms by Truman Capote | $11.00 | 0-679-74564-5 |
| ___ The Fat Man in History by Peter Carey | $10.00 | 0-679-74332-4 |
| ___ The Tax Inspector by Peter Carey | $11.00 | 0-679-73598-4 |
| ___ Bullet Park by John Cheever | $10.00 | 0-679-73787-1 |
| ___ Falconer by John Cheever | $11.00 | 0-679-73786-3 |
| ___ Oh What a Paradise It Seems by John Cheever | $8.00 | 0-679-73785-5 |
| ___ The Wapshot Chronicle by John Cheever | $11.00 | 0-679-73899-1 |
| ___ The Wapshot Scandal by John Cheever | $11.00 | 0-679-73900-9 |
| ___ No Telephone to Heaven by Michelle Cliff | $11.00 | 0-679-73942-4 |
| ___ Age of Iron by J.M. Coetzee | $10.00 | 0-679-73292-6 |
| ___ After Henry by Joan Didion | $12.00 | 0-679-74539-4 |
| ___ Run River by Joan Didion | $11.00 | 0-679-75250-1 |
| ___ Salvador by Joan Didion | $9.00 | 0-679-75183-1 |
| ___ Anecdotes of Destiny and Ehrengard<br>by Isak Dinesen | $12.00 | 0-679-74333-2 |
| ___ Last Tales by Isak Dinesen | $13.00 | 0-679-73640-9 |
| ___ Out of Africa and Shadows on the Grass<br>by Isak Dinesen | $12.00 | 0-679-72475-3 |
| ___ Seven Gothic Tales by Isak Dinesen | $12.00 | 0-679-73641-7 |
| ___ Winter's Tales by Isak Dinesen | $12.00 | 0-679-74334-0 |
| ___ The Book of Daniel by E.L. Doctorow | $10.00 | 0-679-73657-3 |
| ___ Loon Lake by E.L. Doctorow | $10.00 | 0-679-73625-5 |
| ___ Ragtime by E.L. Doctorow | $11.00 | 0-679-73626-3 |
| ___ Welcome to Hard Times by E.L. Doctorow | $10.00 | 0-679-73627-1 |
| ___ World's Fair by E.L. Doctorow | $11.00 | 0-679-73628-X |
| ___ Love, Pain, and the Whole Damn Thing<br>by Doris Dörrie | $9.00 | 0-679-72992-5 |
| ___ The Assignment by Friedrich Dürrenmatt | $7.95 | 0-679-72233-5 |
| ___ Invisible Man by Ralph Ellison | $10.00 | 0-679-72313-7 |
| ___ Scandal by Shusaku Endo | $10.00 | 0-679-72355-2 |
| ___ Absalom, Absalom! by William Faulkner | $9.95 | 0-679-73218-7 |

| | | |
|---|---|---|
| ___ As I Lay Dying by William Faulkner | $9.00 | 0-679-73225-X |
| ___ Big Woods by William Faulkner | $9.00 | 0-679-75252-8 |
| ___ Go Down, Moses by William Faulkner | $10.00 | 0-679-73217-9 |
| ___ The Hamlet by William Faulkner | $10.00 | 0-679-73653-0 |
| ___ Intruder in the Dust by William Faulkner | $9.00 | 0-679-73651-4 |
| ___ Light in August by William Faulkner | $10.00 | 0-679-73226-8 |
| ___ The Reivers by William Faulkner | $10.00 | 0-679-74192-5 |
| ___ Sanctuary by William Faulkner | $10.00 | 0-679-74814-8 |
| ___ The Sound and the Fury by William Faulkner | $9.00 | 0-679-73224-1 |
| ___ The Unvanquished by William Faulkner | $9.00 | 0-679-73652-2 |
| ___ The Good Soldier by Ford Madox Ford | $10.00 | 0-679-72218-1 |
| ___ Howards End by E. M. Forster | $10.00 | 0-679-72255-6 |
| ___ The Longest Journey by E. M. Forster | $11.00 | 0-679-74815-6 |
| ___ A Room With a View by E. M. Forster | $9.00 | 0-679-72476-1 |
| ___ Where Angels Fear to Tread by E. M. Forster | $9.00 | 0-679-73634-4 |
| ___ Christopher Unborn by Carlos Fuentes | $14.00 | 0-679-73222-5 |
| ___ The Story of My Wife by Milán Füst | $8.95 | 0-679-72217-3 |
| ___ The Story of a Shipwrecked Sailor | $9.00 | 0-679-72205-X |
| by Gabriel García Márquez | | |
| ___ The Tin Drum by Günter Grass | $15.00 | 0-679-72575-X |
| ___ Claudius the God by Robert Graves | $14.00 | 0-679-72573-3 |
| ___ I, Claudius by Robert Graves | $12.00 | 0-679-72477-X |
| ___ Dispatches by Michael Herr | $11.00 | 0-679-73525-9 |
| ___ Walter Winchell by Michael Herr | $9.00 | 0-679-73393-0 |
| ___ The Swimming-Pool Library | $12.00 | 0-679-72256-4 |
| by Alan Hollinghurst | | |
| ___ I Served the King of England | $12.00 | 0-679-72786-8 |
| by Bohumil Hrabal | | |
| ___ An Artist of the Floating World | $10.00 | 0-679-72266-1 |
| by Kazuo Ishiguro | | |
| ___ A Pale View of Hills by Kazuo Ishiguro | $10.00 | 0-679-72267-X |
| ___ The Remains of the Day by Kazuo Ishiguro | $11.00 | 0-679-73172-5 |
| ___ A Neil Jordan Reader by Neil Jordan | $12.00 | 0-679-74834-2 |
| ___ Dubliners by James Joyce | $10.00 | 0-679-73990-4 |
| ___ A Portrait of the Artist as a Young Man | $9.00 | 0-679-73989-0 |
| by James Joyce | | |
| ___ Ulysses by James Joyce | $15.00 | 0-679-72276-9 |
| ___ The Emperor by Ryszard Kapuściński | $9.00 | 0-679-72203-3 |
| ___ Shah of Shahs by Ryszard Kapuściński | $10.00 | 0-679-73801-0 |
| ___ The Soccer War by Ryszard Kapuściński | $10.00 | 0-679-73805-3 |
| ___ China Men by Maxine Hong Kingston | $10.00 | 0-679-72328-5 |
| ___ Tripmaster Monkey by Maxine Hong Kingston | $11.00 | 0-679-72789-2 |
| ___ The Woman Warrior by Maxine Hong Kingston | $10.00 | 0-679-72188-6 |
| ___ Judge on Trial by Ivan Klíma | $14.00 | 0-679-73756-1 |
| ___ Love and Garbage by Ivan Klíma | $11.00 | 0-679-73755-3 |
| ___ Barabbas by Pär Lagerkvist | $8.00 | 0-679-72544-X |
| ___ The Plumed Serpent by D. H. Lawrence | $12.00 | 0-679-73493-7 |
| ___ The Virgin & the Gipsy by D. H. Lawrence | $10.00 | 0-679-74077-5 |
| ___ The Radiance of the King by Camara Laye | $12.00 | 0-679-72200-9 |
| ___ Canopus in Argos by Doris Lessing | $20.00 | 0-679-74184-4 |
| ___ The Fifth Child by Doris Lessing | $9.00 | 0-679-72182-7 |

# VINTAGE INTERNATIONAL

# VINTAGE INTERNATIONAL

| | | |
|---|---|---|
| ___ **Pale Fire** by Vladimir Nabokov | $11.00 | 0-679-72342-0 |
| ___ **Pnin** by Vladimir Nabokov | $10.00 | 0-679-72341-2 |
| ___ **The Real Life of Sebastian Knight** by Vladimir Nabokov | $10.00 | 0-679-72726-4 |
| ___ **Speak, Memory** by Vladimir Nabokov | $12.00 | 0-679-72339-0 |
| ___ **Strong Opinions** by Vladimir Nabokov | $12.00 | 0-679-72609-8 |
| ___ **Transparent Things** by Vladimir Nabokov | $10.00 | 0-679-72541-5 |
| ___ **A Bend in the River** by V. S. Naipaul | $10.00 | 0-679-72202-5 |
| ___ **Guerrillas** by V. S. Naipaul | $10.95 | 0-679-73174-1 |
| ___ **A Turn in the South** by V. S. Naipaul | $11.00 | 0-679-72488-5 |
| ___ **The English Patient** by Michael Ondaatje | $11.00 | 0-679-74520-3 |
| ___ **Running in the Family** by Michael Ondaatje | $10.00 | 0-679-74669-2 |
| ___ **Body Snatcher** by Juan Carlos Onetti | $13.00 | 0-679-73887-8 |
| ___ **Black Box** by Amos Oz | $11.00 | 0-679-72185-1 |
| ___ **My Michael** by Amos Oz | $11.00 | 0-679-72804-X |
| ___ **The Slopes of Lebanon** by Amos Oz | $11.00 | 0-679-73144-X |
| ___ **Metaphor and Memory** by Cynthia Ozick | $13.00 | 0-679-73425-2 |
| ___ **The Shawl** by Cynthia Ozick | $7.95 | 0-679-72926-7 |
| ___ **Dictionary of the Khazars** by Milorad Pavić | | |
|     male edition | $12.00 | 0-679-72461-3 |
|     female edition | $12.00 | 0-679-72754-X |
| ___ **Truck Stop Rainbows** by Iva Pekárková | $11.00 | 0-679-74675-7 |
| ___ **Cambridge** by Caryl Phillips | $10.00 | 0-679-73689-1 |
| ___ **The Law of White Spaces** by Giorgio Pressburger | $10.00 | 0-679-75246-3 |
| ___ **Complete Collected Stories** by V. S. Pritchett | $20.00 | 0-679-73892-4 |
| ___ **Swann's Way** by Marcel Proust | $13.00 | 0-679-72009-X |
| ___ **Kiss of the Spider Woman** by Manuel Puig | $11.00 | 0-679-72449-4 |
| ___ **Memoirs of an Anti-Semite** by Gregor von Rezzori | $12.00 | 0-679-73182-2 |
| ___ **The Orient-Express** by Gregor von Rezzori | $11.00 | 0-679-74822-9 |
| ___ **The Snows of Yesteryear** by Gregor von Rezzori | $10.95 | 0-679-73181-4 |
| ___ **The Notebooks of Malte Laurids Brigge** by Rainer Maria Rilke | $12.00 | 0-679-73245-4 |
| ___ **Selected Poetry** by Rainer Maria Rilke | $12.00 | 0-679-72201-7 |
| ___ **The Breast** by Philip Roth | $9.00 | 0-679-74901-2 |
| ___ **Goodbye, Columbus** by Philip Roth | $11.00 | 0-679-74826-1 |
| ___ **My Life as a Man** by Philip Roth | $11.00 | 0-679-74827-X |
| ___ **Operation Shylock** by Philip Roth | $12.00 | 0-679-75029-0 |
| ___ **The Professor of Desire** by Philip Roth | $10.00 | 0-679-74900-4 |
| ___ **Mating** by Norman Rush | $12.00 | 0-679-73709-X |
| ___ **Whites** by Norman Rush | $9.00 | 0-679-73816-9 |
| ___ **The Age of Reason** by Jean-Paul Sartre | $12.00 | 0-679-73895-9 |
| ___ **No Exit and 3 Other Plays** by Jean-Paul Sartre | $10.00 | 0-679-72516-4 |
| ___ **The Reprieve** by Jean-Paul Sartre | $12.00 | 0-679-74078-3 |
| ___ **Troubled Sleep** by Jean-Paul Sartre | $12.00 | 0-679-74079-1 |
| ___ **Open Doors and Three Novellas** by Leonardo Sciascia | $12.00 | 0-679-73561-5 |
| ___ **Cock and Bull** by Will Self | $11.00 | 0-679-75092-4 |
| ___ **All You Who Sleep Tonight** by Vikram Seth | $7.00 | 0-679-73025-7 |
| ___ **The Golden Gate** by Vikram Seth | $13.00 | 0-679-73457-0 |
| ___ **And Quiet Flows the Don** by Mikhail Sholokhov | $15.00 | 0-679-72521-0 |

# VINTAGE INTERNATIONAL

___ **By Grand Central Station I Sat Down and Wept**    $10.00    0-679-73804-5
     by Elizabeth Smart
___ **Ake: The Years of Childhood** by Wole Soyinka    $12.00    0-679-72540-7
___ **Ìsarà: A Voyage Around "Essay"**    $9.95    0-679-73246-2
     by Wole Soyinka
___ **Children of Light** by Robert Stone    $10.00    0-679-73593-3
___ **A Flag for Sunrise** by Robert Stone    $12.00    0-679-73762-6
___ **Confessions of Nat Turner** by William Styron    $12.00    0-679-73663-8
___ **Lie Down in Darkness** by William Styron    $12.00    0-679-73597-6
___ **The Long March** and **In the Clap Shack**    $11.00    0-679-73675-1
     by William Styron
___ **Set This House on Fire** by William Styron    $12.00    0-679-73674-3
___ **Sophie's Choice** by William Styron    $13.00    0-679-73637-9
___ **This Quiet Dust** by William Styron    $12.00    0-679-73596-8
___ **Confessions of Zeno** by Italo Svevo    $12.00    0-679-72234-3
___ **Ever After** by Graham Swift    $11.00    0-679-74026-0
___ **Learning to Swim** by Graham Swift    $9.00    0-679-73978-5
___ **Out of This World** by Graham Swift    $10.00    0-679-74032-5
___ **Shuttlecock** by Graham Swift    $10.00    0-679-73933-5
___ **The Sweet-Shop Owner** by Graham Swift    $10.00    0-679-73980-7
___ **Waterland** by Graham Swift    $11.00    0-679-73979-3
___ **The Beautiful Mrs. Seidenman**    $9.95    0-679-73214-4
     by Andrzej Szczypiorski
___ **Diary of a Mad Old Man** by Junichiro Tanizaki    $10.00    0-679-73024-9
___ **The Key** by Junichiro Tanizaki    $11.00    0-679-73023-0
___ **On the Golden Porch** by Tatyana Tolstaya    $11.00    0-679-72843-0
___ **Sleepwalker in a Fog** by Tatyana Tolstaya    $10.00    0-679-73063-X
___ **The Real Life of Alejandro Mayta**    $12.00    0-679-72478-8
     by Mario Vargas Llosa
___ **The Eye of the Story** by Eudora Welty    $8.95    0-679-73004-4
___ **Losing Battles** by Eudora Welty    $11.00    0-679-72882-1
___ **The Optimist's Daughter** by Eudora Welty    $9.00    0-679-72883-X
___ **The Passion** by Jeanette Winterson    $10.00    0-679-72437-0
___ **Sexing the Cherry** by Jeanette Winterson    $10.00    0-679-73316-7
___ **Written on the Body** by Jeanette Winterson    · $11.00    0-679-74447-9